The Naked Detective & the Movies

A Book & Page
Nottinghill Lane Mystery
Book 3

by Guy Veryzer

c 2019 - rev 10/12/21

This book is dedicated to
Movies
Small towns,
Background Actors
- who get little credit
and the lovers
of mysteries.

Contents

Prologue - A Unexpected Body 5

Chapter 1 - A Dinosaur Comes to Town..................... 9

Chapter 2 - Are the Stars Out Tonight? 18

Chapter 3 - The Reality of Make Believe................... 30

Chapter 4 - The Plot 43

Chapter 5 - Holding.. 51

Chapter 6 - Willing Prisoner 68

Chapter 7 - Professional Users................................... 83

Chapter 8 - The Hooded Phantom............................ 97

Chapter 9 - The First Body.. 107

Chapter 10 - Un-murder ....
123

Chapter 11 - Uninsurable Nightmare ....
131

Chapter 12 - Stand Ins ....
143

Chapter 13 - Lights, Camera, Budget ....
153

Chapter 14 - Shot in the Dark ....
166

Chapter 15 - Movie Mosaic ....
180

Chapter 16 - Multiple Personalities ....
191

Chapter 17 - Another Body ....
204

Chapter 18 - Deadly Friendship ....
217

Chapter 19 - Invisible Visible ....
228

Chapter 20 - A Party & A Viper Lover ....
239

Epilogue ....
246

4

The movies…are a kingdom.

They say the class system doesn't exist any more,
which is nonsense, it is many places,
most especially the movie world,
each film set
is as ranked a royal cast system
as Versailles ever was…

Prologue - A Unexpected Body

In Hollywood California, it was very early in the morning, 4:30 AM on location for filming a new mystery movie Dead of Night - starring major film star Cal Radcliffe.

It was the third week of filming, they were on schedule and since setting the lights was taking longer than usual, the techs were in extra early to load in equipment.

"Wow, those prop guys are on top of things, I didn't think they'd put the dead body in place until later before we begin to shoot," Mel, one of the lightning crew, said to another.

"Huh, I'd have thought they'd have finished dressing the set before bringing it in," Nelson, another lighting man said, as he carefully stacked light-stands off to one side of the old drugstore that they were shooting in that day. There were a lot of filters and boxes of gels already stacked. "It's gonna take Andre's special touch to get the lighting flattering enough to make the star look young."

What looked like the body of a woman was sprawled on the floor next to the prescription counter. There was blood pooling from her blonde hair.

"That's strange; they don't usually place the blood till right before we shoot."

The two men stepped nearer to peer down more closely.

They looked at each other with expressions of slowly dawning shock as the realization struck them both that this was no prop body, this was real blood, this was in fact...

Nelson gasped, "This is an actual dead body, a corpse."

"Yeah, I think that's kinda how it works, corpses are dead. But what's she doing here?" Mel wondered, right before he fainted.

* * *

The movie managed to hush up the dead body scandal, which continued to be an unsolved mystery.

However the film was not a success at the box-office, another in a string of failures for the movie star. Cal Radcliffe needed a new film project and he wanted to get away from Hollywood for a while. He had a script, a script with his name on it, with a leading part for him.

It just happened that Michigan was offering huge tax incentives for the movie business to come to the state. It also happened there was a picturesque little lakeside town that was a perfect location for Cal Radcliffe's next film, a place called Bluewater.

The casting director told Cal he'd discovered there was an actor living in the town, who might be right for a part in the film, a former TV star not — just a local, "A cute guy and he'll save us money!"

Cal's eyes gleamed as he gazed at the image of the handsome young man.

Chapter 1 - A Dinosaur Comes to Town

Over the long cold winter, artist Jack Page and detective Michael Book, the handsome young occupants of the Nottinghill Lane carriage house, had enjoyed short frosty busy days and long warm cozy nights. Like the other residents of their Lane they had been well stocked with books to read, and blizzards had canceled only a few of their monthly bookclub meetings, but they were all defiantly ready for the long awaited change of season.

Bluewater City had shivered through the many winter months, spring would come, after all it was April, however, as this was teasing and taunting northern Michigan, where sun would shine bright and warm, then suddenly snow would fall again, then depart, only to come back like a slap in the face...then, maybe...finally, icicles and snow piles would diminish. Just as everyone's patience was running out, there would be tiny green possibilities sprouting up here and there on muddy swaths of land, as fields and gardens were slowly waking, as the blankets of snow were finally, gradually, vanishing.

At the end of a week of changeable spring weather, with a new still-life painting completed by Jack, and a missing person's case solved by Detective Mike, the pair were catching up with each other over dinner by the fire.

"Hey, Jack, did you hear there's going to be a movie shooting in town?" Mike said to his lover as they were eating a tasty Italian meal prepared by the chef of the pair, who not only was a good cook, an amateur magician, and model for his artist partner, but in his day job, Mike was a small town police detective. That was how he heard about the movie since there were city permits that were required as well as police assistance.

"Well, there certainly are a lot of great locations to use as background and settings in this area," Jack said, reaching to refill their wine glasses with Chianti, which poured out as a rich ruby color in the candlelight.

"You don't seem very excited."

"Been there, done that," Jack responded. He then happily savored his mouth full of dinner. He loved his partner's cooking, "This pasta is different, I like it...and you've done the meatballs with basil and mmmm, something else, I like them, too."

"Thank you very much," Mike said, his green cat eyes gleaming in the flames light.

"What?" Jack asked. "Mike, you've got a look like you're not telling me something. What is it?"

Mike smiled and answered, "Well, it's just...the meatballs are meatless and the pasta is edamame...made from soybeans. I wanted to see what I could make when we have vegetarians over for dinner."

"Wow, well, it still tastes great," Jack grinned.

"Jack, now it's you who looks like you have something you're not saying..."

"Well, it's not about your food, it's delicious. But since you mentioned the movie, well, as it happens, I did get a call from my agent. He knows about the film, and knows I'm local. The casting people have been reaching out, it doesn't have a huge budget, so if they could find local talent with a track record..."

"They offered you a part?" Mike asked eagerly.

"Well, it's more like an offer to offer me a part. It would just be a small part. And it would be using my stage name, so if, I say if, I did it, I'm hoping no one will notice."

"But that could be great!"

"Why great?" Jack asked, surprised at his reaction.

"Well, because officers from the department are supposed to work on the film with traffic, making sure safety regulations are followed. There's a chance I might be asked to consult as a detective."

Jack took a sip of his wine; they both did, as they thought about what might be good, and what might be bad about working on this movie, a film production in their area, in their very own town.

Jack knew from past experience film productions were like dinosaurs, or King Kong. They move in, everyone gets excited, they take over, and you don't know what they will leave behind when they move on.

"Jack, do you know what the movie's about?" Mike asked.

"I think it's a murder mystery," he said.

14

* * *

Jack: Even before the spring was near, our young garden designer Hank had, been emailing plans and design drawings for a little project Mike had in mind to add to his culinary advancement. Partly for a summer course credit, partly for money, and partly for his pure love of landscaping, - Hank was going to help create an herb and vegetable garden for us, so Mike can source things for his delicious gastronomic adventures only steps outside our backdoor.

Hank was suggesting creating tiers, like steps along the inside of the West fence of the house garden, (so it would get the East morning sun). His designs included making some trellis works to give a sculptural effect to some of the plantings, and putting in very attractive configurations of colors of vegetables so that view from the studio would be inviting.

Having young, good-looking Hank working in shorts with his abs flexing under his T-shirt would be a nice view as well.

He had written saying this summer he would be augmented by a crew of one, a new collage friend from his landscaping course named Greer who he'd invited to help him. He wanted to clear it with Mike and me beforehand, as in addition to the house garden, we had a large hidden garden, behind that garden...a secret beautiful, well camouflaged sanctuary, shared with a select few of Nottinghill Lane neighbors.

Mike and I talked it over, and Hank had done an amazing job on the hidden gardens over the past summer and even helping on weekends far into the fall.

He'd been very discreet, even making up a fantasy location for the images he used in his presentation for school, to guard the secret. We thought if he trusted this friend Greer, that was a good sign. But I emailed him, not to clue his friend in until he'd been around us for a while to check him out. Hank totally understood and totally agreed.

Mike and I were curious as to what this Greer would look like. If he had even a fraction of Hank's model good looks, well...that would be extra fun. It would re-double the eye candy, although it might drive cute nerdy Justin up a wall, right up a garden wall, as he could either be jealous of Hank (his unrequited love) or have twice as many boy-crushes. Although with the movie coming into town could distract Justin, especially if there were cute actors.

I mentioned to Hank in email about possible movie shooting in town, just to warn him that Mike and I will be a little busy, and he would be fairly autonomous. Hank refreshingly, seemed totally uninterested in the production, other than saying he hoped it wouldn't cause too many traffic problems.

I had thought maybe he'd be interested in working with the art director, or scenic designer people if they need to landscape outdoor locations. But Hank didn't ask, so I didn't bring it up.

I have a feeling I will have enough on my hands with Justin and Chelsea who are already badgering me with questions and soon may be angling to get involved with the film somehow.

I am very glad my role would be very small, at least in the script I saw. Which I am sure is constantly changing, as everything in movie making does. I was told it took five years to Green-light this project and it may take a year before it will be edited and realized, and that's only a maybe, nothing is certain in this business.

It is too early to see any kind of shooting breakdown, but my hope is my scenes would all be done in a few days in a row, and I can hide away from the rest of the production in my safe little world of Nottinghill Lane.

Little did I know.

Chapter 2 - Are the Stars Out Tonight?

The movie was titled: Songbird Murders, a script that the writer-producer Jerry McBride had in turnaround until he had it reworked to fit its two name stars. Once the big names signed on, it was finally a go.

It was a small budget film, (which is still millions of dollars) and there was a lot of production talent, hoping to give it an edgy creativity that could refocus everyone's careers.

A small town American murder mystery might even have big international appeal. Plus both stars still had loyal European and Asian fans.

Jessica Zane had been a successful actress for 10 years, at thirty-two she was getting nervous; it was a tricky age in the business. It had been a few films since she'd been in a hit. Hits were harder to come by; the entertainment industry had changed so radically in recent years. She was hoping she could land a streaming series, now that they were as prestigious at films, she was hoping she could work in one place. She was tired of the gypsy life of camping on films...

* * *

"I think you're gorgeous!" the beautiful movie star said to her reflection in the mirror of her hotel room. The slender red-haired woman thought about having a drink, it was a bit early in the day, even for her.

Jessica mused that so far this location seemed like it could be pleasant, a lakeside small town. Not many paparazzi would come to this remote part of the Northwest. Local small town papers and fans would be much easier and controllable, she thought — she hoped. Though she knew that all the lies and rumors the junk press made up about her, actually helped her celebrity to some degree...and helped hide her secret.

Her personal assistant knew the truth, but she was her protector. Jes was so grateful for Whitney, she could do everything, like a girl wizard...like for example, the banks of makeup lights that were at the moment making her look good in the dressing table in this quaint hotel room. Wit had managed to materialize them and install them for her like magic.

Jessica decided she might have just one little glass of whiskey while she looked over the latest script revisions, what color were the newest ones? Pink? Green? The script was starting to look like a rainbow.

The production company had rented out the entire hotel, The Blue Swan. It was historic, and they would be doing a lot of shooting here. A few of the of the top people living here, in the hotels old world, somewhat faded elegance, housed on the third floor well away from the noise, but close at hand. The lesser crew people would be lodged down the road at a motel, and there were local hires as well.

It was a fine suite of rooms for the moment, Jessica appreciated its Edwardian decor. She liked the ornate molded plaster details and all the rose colored damask velvet. The actress swathed in wine color velvet robe lounged with her shapely legs curled up under her on the antique chaise lounge in the bay window that looked out over the lake, she breathed in the cool breeze that fluttered the lace curtains, and she sipped her crystal tumbler of liquid fire, and focused on her pages. Her script trembled in her hand slightly, she propped a cushion under it and swore softly.

Cal's part seemed to be getting larger and hers smaller in one of her favorite scenes. She had worked with Cal only once before, years ago, they had gotten along then. He had never tried to bed her, but that was no surprise to her…he had been making it with the young actor playing her brother in the film.

She thought of her assistant Whitney who was excited that Charlie Robin - former child actor, whose real name Jack Book has a part in this project. Growing up she had loved the show he was on USA Family, She had a memory of him as a cute kid.

Jessica thought, it will be interesting, maybe scary to see what he's grown up to be. Kid actors can go either way, if they manage to even stay in the business.

"If he's grown up cute, I'm sure Cal will have an eye on him, or two eyes…and a hand, or two, " she murmured to herself.

She thought she could handle Cal. If she had any problems with him, she could always tell her faithful Whitney, and the girl could work her magic. Jess sipped her whisky and thought about magic.

* * *

Whitney Sims prided herself on being the best personal assistant in the business. She had studied both business and interior design at Parsons in New York; she had also dabbled in art and Victorian literature. Wit had grown up in a well-to-do Connecticut family. One summer, Jessica Zane was working in a movie in Greenwich. It happened the movie production was using a house nearby as a location for the wedding which was the main action of the film. Through nepotistic connections, Whitney's mother's — brother's — wife's — cousin was a script supervisor on the movie. So it worked out Whitney assisted her cousin in law; Jasper Stone, a publicist.

In the course of her many errands during the movie shoot, Whitney solved a number of little issues for Jessica Zane's assistant Jill - an aspiring screenwriter, when suddenly her script got the green light finally, after five years, Jill had suggested Witney to replace her.

Jessica had been a favorite and inspiration to Wit, since the two films she loved, Blonde Ambition, and Blonde Justice, in which a smart young woman works her way through law school to win huge legal cases in the small firm she starts, then in the second film becomes a Supreme Court judge.

The assistant suggested capable, cute Whitney to Jessica who had liked Whitney, especially as she said she had no interest in acting. Also the fact Wit was a bit full figured, making Jesica feel thiner, was an extra perk.

From then on Whitney had been on a mission to be indispensable. Though much younger than Jessica, she often felt like a mama bird, nurturing and feathering the nest of "her star".

Her interior design skills came into play in her ornamenting or beautifying the various dressing rooms, trailers, and living accommodations for her patron, as Wit thought of her employer.

In their present period hotel, she had made sure to get images of the rooms of the suite in advance, and sent drawings and instructions ahead of how to rearrange things. She also shipped linens, towels and various personal things ahead to be put in place.

Outsiders might think such details diva like, but when a person spends months on end away from home, having things you're used to is comforting and less unsettling. It was Wits job to keep Jessica at her best and she did so extremely well.

As she looked up from her laptop in the smaller room next door to Jessica's, pausing from her to do lists, she enjoyed the view of the sapphire waters and waves meeting blue sky. With the white sails of boats skimming here and there, it was something Impressionists would have painted.

Her mind rested momentarily on the thought

she was going to meet the former star of USA Family... one of them. She had read they were twins, but the one who was going to work in the film, who she heard actually lived nearby...She had seen Jack in some of his short-lived later projects as a teen, she always thought he'd needed better material. Then he seemed to disappear, so she wondered if this was a comeback for him? He was her same age, that was partly why she'd found him so interesting. She wondered what he looked like now, what he'd been doing. She hoped he wasn't another ex-child actor rehab alumni.

She had learned it was usually better not to meet Stars you admired in person, (Jessica being an exception) but she was curious. He has several scenes with Jess.

* * *

The male lead of the film was actor Cal Radcliffe. He was considered a topnotch actor, and the name that got the picture green lit.

Cal was not however, a handsome heartthrob. He was average looking, with a receding hairline, but his eyes and smile could dazzle, or look dangerous, combined with his ceaseless networking and his talent he remained a star. Sometimes Cal shined bright enough to catch an oscar, at the moment his star shine was dimmer, hoping this film would have a successful gleam.

Nonetheless Cal was still constantly photographed dating beautiful women, (still unmarried at 48) while in the business it was an open secret all his sexual affairs were with young men.

Cal focused like a laser on any role he was acting, but he got bored being himself and he didn't like boredom. So when he found himself with time on his hands on movie sets, he enjoyed distracting himself with having his hands occupied with whatever cute young guy was handy and willing. If they weren't so willing at first, his charm and his offer of connections in the business soon undressed most hot aspiring day players, or production assistants who wanted to direct.

If Cal was tired, he could always have his personal assistant shop the extras holding for eye candy, bring him their headshots and he could do some auditions in his trailer. If a young actor upgraded Cal, he might get them upgraded. Extras would kill each other to get just one line, and he'd be happy to give them one line, as long the line they read for him was 'Yes'.

Besides the easy pickings of l*ow hanging fruit* as Cal privately called his one off tricks, Cal liked the challenge of the long game, a hot guy who seemed like they would never say yes to him.

* * *

Jack had heard all about Cal's reputation, Jack would never say yes to Cal which he would make clear politely, and professionally. But looking as handsome as Jack did he would definitely get on

Cal's challenge list, as would his drop dead gorgeous boyfriend, Detective Mike. And if Cal ever saw their young friend Hank stop by the set, Zoom! Right to the top of the challenge list Hank would fly.

Chapter 3 - The Reality of Make Believe

Mike: Jack is pretending he's not nervous about working on this film. He said it's just a small part, which will probably be cut to nothing in editing. But I can tell he wants to be good, he's a quality guy, whatever he does he wants to be good, constantly practicing to improve, with his artwork, his gardening, his new found love of reading and writing... and with us, being in a relationship is work, learning and practice.

And Lordy I love our practice sessions!

* * *

Jack: I think Mike is worried about me being worried about acting. Which is not what I am worried about. I know what to do, and I am not out to win an academy award. This film project is just something that came my way and I thought it might be interesting to work with Jessica and Cal.

What I am worried about is my privacy, our privacy, and the little world we have on Nottinghill Lane.

Even though I will be using my stage name, it will still come out who I am and where…Unless…

Maybe I could be my brother Daniel. I should give him a call and ask if he would let me be him? Or maybe I could get him to be me, and he could come up here and visit. Though he is so off the grid and happy in his rural mountain world in Virginia.

Anyway, that's what I'm concerned with. Mike and Justin and Chelsea...basically everyone in town is keen on this movie...Is it weird that I have no worries about my gay relationship coming out, but coming out here as an actor is what scares me?

I'm glad the film company is renting the Blue Swan Hotel, it's been in real financial trouble, this could help it a lot. The timing couldn't be better, since it needed a lot of renovation. Anyway, the production company can do what they like and it will all be refurbished afterwards.

Mike and I had been given a tour of the place by Ned Orton the manager, one night when we had dinner there. They have a good whitefish special Thursdays. Hemingway used to drink at the bar, but then they tell you that at any bar in northern Michigan that was around in the 1930s. Still the place has atmosphere.

It should be just the right atmosphere for this story, of a handsome young man accused of murdering three women, the feisty lawyer who defends him, the sheriff who believes he's guilty, and his young deputy who thinks maybe he's not. Add to the plot the woman DA and the Defense lawyer used to be collage sweethearts.

The young deputy, that would be my part.

Cal Radcliffe is the gentle but gritty lawyer, Jessica plays the singing District Attorney. The judge for the court room scene was going to be the great old actor Brandon Walters.

* * *

The script reading was held in the party room of a restaurant behind the old hotel that was the main hub of production. The cast of the film was not large, two leads and five principle players. The script supervisor named: Kat was going to read stage directions and any under-five (very minor parts) as well as making any necessary notes.

Once everyone in the cast was assembled and took their seats at the long table, script pages rattled and rustled. Then there was an expectant hush.

The director James Barker, was a tall grasshopper of a man, with a short silver beard and yachting cap which would have seemed very affected if he didn't seem so much a ship captain. His deep commanding voice was so assured it demanded to be heard and obeyed. He explained, "We are going to be shooting the courtroom scenes first as they require the entire cast, and extras. We'll be shooting first in a former church that has been restyled. Meanwhile the set designer and dresser will work on the hotels locations. The hotel where the majority of the small scenes take place would be in process of staging while we shoot the court room. But before that we shoot the exteriors before it begins to be tourist season."

"Now in the script the courtroom is the penultimate scene, but we need to shoot that first. I am now thinking of coverage that might start the film as the trial starts, the fade into flashback retelling the events preceding it, or maybe not. It's all about possibilities."

"That's right JB. possibilities," The AD (assistant director) echoed.

"So keep that in mind as we read through, and when we shoot, I will want takes with different emotional colors."

"Lots of colors," the AD echoed again.

Cal smiled at Jessica, "OK Jess, let's be colorful you murdering songbird!"

Smiling back at him she said, "I'll be an acting rainbow!"

Everyone chuckled. Then we read through the courtroom scenes.

I had a few lines on the stand being cross examined, about finding the body of the first murder victim by the lake. One of my lines was: "I'm not a medical examiner, but he sure looked dead to me sir." The line earned me a big laugh, which I'm not sure was the scripts intention. But Jessica smiled at me with approval.

After the first script read through of the new scenes I thought the potential for a real life murder were almost as high as the ones in the movie script.

The director, Barker, was very animated at first welcoming everyone, once the read through began he was preoccupied with going over the shot lists and storyboards as he listened to the loose read-through, picturing in his mind the overall flow of the film as he listened.

Off to the side of the room, sat the first AD (assistant director), and the second AD who was almost invisible huddled at his laptop confining schedules and locations and various budget issues...contracts and so on. The Second-second, as the assistant to the assistant-assistant director was called...he was not the easiest guy, but got results.

Jessica was nervous but it didn't stop her from giving a wonderful reading of her character. She even sang a little of the song her character performs in the hotel lounge.

Cal's reading was good, but he was very restrained. I know some actors don't like to give too much unless the camera is rolling. Afterwards he acted sweet, but acting is what he does... I didn't fully buy it. I bet he gives his assistant hell behind closed doors. Speaking of closed doors, I wouldn't want the doors to be closed and be alone with him, he undresses me with his eyes enough already. I wouldn't want to experience the real event.

* * *

"How'd it go?" Mike asked when I got home. I hugged Mike and said, "Oh it was fine, but it's such a crazy bubble. I need a dose of normal...or a glass of something."

"Coming right up," Mike smiled and poured us both white wine, and he led me to the kitchen counter where he proceeded to amuse me with his magic skills by materializing ingredients from out of nowhere, an empty mixing bowl suddenly had a half dozen eggs in it. He juggled big Portobello mushrooms which suddenly disappeared...

Then Mike rapidly carved tiny faces in some red potatoes and with napkins for bodies he performed a little puppet show! He told jokes as he chopped onions and herbs. Then my magic chief climaxed his amusing kitchen show with a rapid fire sizzling and tossing of pans over burners on the stove. Almost instantly perfect omelets and crisp brown fried potatoes were plated before my dazzled eyes.

I was afraid he was going to juggle again with the plates or make them disappear, but instead he asked me to carry them out to the table on the garden patio, as he followed with a green salad.

Looking at my handsome magician lover across the candlelight, his green eyes glowing like marbles, I felt like the luckiest guy in the world.

Mike hadn't had time to change out of his work suit. Todays was a dark grey one. He'd managed to do all that cooking performance in a suit! Maybe it gave him pockets to hide things in...As he slipped his jacket off putting it over the back of his chair, I saw he even still had his shoulder holster on, however when he sat, I saw it wasn't holding his pistol, instead he pulled out a pepper grinder.

I chuckled as he garnished our dinner with spice. "Mike I asked for a dose of normal not The Houdini Cooking show."

"Hey, this is the new normal," he grinned looking ten years old. He toasted me and I toasted him back.

"Well, you certainly distracted me, and cleared my head of movie angst." I took a bite of the Portobello omelet, "Wow, this is omelet is truly magic!"

I sighed and chewed happily, then swallowed and said, "And what a beautiful evening."

Gazing around at the few early flowers mixed with tall decorative grasses gently swaying in the dusk breeze. With the tall vine covered fence and trees encircling the lovely yard, I felt we were alone together in a small paradise. Stars were watching us, reflecting in the small pond nearby.

"Nottinghill Lane normal," I sighed.

"So how long do you rehearse?" Mike asked.

"Rehearse?" I scoffed gently, "This isn't the theater. We just jump off and dive in."

"Really? Wow! You just start filming?"

"Well, every film and director is different. There are no rules in the business. Its show business not show art. In movies there are budgets and shot lists and schedules. If you're lucky some art and talent shine through, but art and talent are commodities, jobs just like the lighting crew, set dressers, camera and sound techs. Everyone is hired to do their job as best they can, and as quickly and efficiently."

"Okay, I get it. So the movies aren't like they show making movies in the movies," Mike and I both laughed at how confusing that sounded. But I said, "Exactly."

"You look so young and pretty, and yet you can

sound like an old used car salesman."

"Hey, *mister magical police detective*, you know about the reality behind the tricks."

Sipping his wine, as I savored my last forkful of delicious dinner, Mike pretended to sound affronted, "Please! Illusions, not tricks! Tricks are for card sharks, magicians are masters of illusion."

"Are you going to make these dishes disappear?"

"Certainly, with the help of my talented and attractive assistant we are."

He smiled, "Then we can make our clothes and cares vanish as we shower together, while you tell me more about the dark and dirty world of movies."

"Good thing I don't have an early call time tomorrow, my little scene isn't on the call sheet until after lunch."

"Anyway," I yawned, "a lot of film actors don't want to get stale, lose their spontaneity rehearsing. When I did the teen TV police show, we used to make mistakes on purpose just so we could get to do more than one take."

Mike whispered, "If we rehearse a love scene right now, I don't think that you'll get stale."

"I might fall asleep."

"I'll take that as a challenge," he responded with a seductive smirk.

Our evenings pleasurable magic continued upstairs and it wasn't an illusion.

Rehearsing had never been so much fun.

I didn't fall asleep, until ...much, much later...

Chapter 4 - The Plot

Of course, the members of the Nottinghill Lane Book Club were all desperately wanting to know the story of the movie shooting in town. It was their unanimous decision that Jack tell them the story, or as much of it as he could without violating any secrecy agreement. Many of the colorful group were hoping to work as background players so they would find out a lot about it eventually, but their curiosity overwhelmed their patience.

So, on a Sunday evening everyone gathered at the Inkblot Pub, where they had reserved the backroom and closed the pocket doors to distance from listening ears. All the members were gathered, including; Dr. Dorothy (know as Dot) her partner Janet Baum (*who was Jack's uncle — now his aunt*), antique dealer Roddy Grey and his life size doll companion Alfie, young friends; Chelsea, Justin, Hank and Greer, and the rest of the characters of the book-group.

It took quite a while for everyone to be comfortably seated, for Janet's wheelchair to be well placed, and drinks of choice find their way into everyones hands. Finally an anticipatory hush fell over the small crowd, Jack stood at the end of the table, behind him a window with closed red velvet curtains became his center stage. The waiter dramatically dimmed the room leaving just one small track spot above him. Jack suddenly felt he was giving a theatrical performance as he began to tell the movie story in a his gentle, but clearly audible voice...

"The movie opens with the voiceover of the lawyer who is defending a young murderer...The voice is the deep warm resonant voice of Cal Radcliffe, a star familiar to most people... As the camera zooms over our lovely Rainbow Lake shoreline and over our town of Bluewater... rechristened: Summerville and Crystal Lake for the film.

We zoom over the landscape into our mainstreet and then it zooms in peering through the courthouse window revealing a trial for murder is beginning.

A young man is being accused of strangling three young women, all victims found with red scarves around their necks and each wearing a small gold bird pin.

The prosecuting attorney is a local woman, who also sings on weekends at the hotel lounge. Her role is played by the very talented Jessica Zane.

One interesting twist — the female prosecutor (Jessica) is also a performer, who sings Saturday evenings in the hotel where is the young man accused of the murders worked as a bartender.

The Hotel is where one of the murders took place.

The defense attorney — played by Cal Radcliffe, is a former local who made it big in New York, but has been hired to come back and defend this case because of his local knowledge.

Here's another twist is Cal and Jessica's characters — the prosecutor and the defense attorney were high school sweethearts.

The trial begins with lawyers explaining the case to the jury, (which might be some of you as you all want to be extras...)

This is where I come in, as a witness who was on the scene of the first body found in the waterside park...As I am describing what I saw...

The movie begins to have flashbacks of the story and characters and how the murders played out," Jack picked up his drink and took a well deserved sip.

"Did he do it, the young man accused?" asked Mrs. Darknight, murmured in her Bronte somber voice.

"To be honest, I don't know. They are keeping the ending of the movie secret even from the actors," Jack said.

A voice spoke up from the back of the room, Howard (the Edgar Allen Poe fan) expounded, sounding righteous. "Wait, wait, wait! I read this book called: The Snowfall Murders, is that what this came from? If it is, they changed everything about the book; it's not winter, it was children that were the victims and there was no courtrooms or lawyers..."

Jack shrugged his shoulders, "Howard, what I was told was Cal Radcliffe wrote the screenplay himself with a friend, or so he claims. I wish I had a good answer for you about the book you're talking about."

"Do you have any answer?" The older man huffed tossing his long silver ponytail. He felt, as an aspiring writer himself, that an authors work was sacrosanct and this authors work had been violated.

"Howard, I have an answer for you, but it's not a good one," Annabelle Southern, (the Gone with the Wind Devote) spoke up melodiously drawling her words, "That book, the book you're referring to, was already made into a movie, titled Blood on the Snow. But it was not good, and that film really messed with the authors work."

"It is one of the gambles of selling your book rights to Hollywood," Jack said. "What I can tell you is, authors generally are well paid for the movie rights...but they relinquish all control."

"A deal with the devil," Justin murmured, "but a tempting one." Justin's thoughts seemed to be wandering a bit, as on the word tempting his eyes shot over to Hank who for some time had been the dream-boy of his own romantic scribblings. Hank the very good-looking preppie with a green thumb, had inspired Justin to attempt a graphic novel about a blonde gardener super hero. But it hadn't gone very far. Being much more practically minded and interested in specifics, the budding young writer, red headed Chelsea, (who still deciding between reporter and spy) asked, "How much do the novel rights go for? Millions?   Jack looked around the room at the many interested faces... "Well...maybe, maybe for Comic book franchises...Novels, I'm guessing five or six figures. But I'm exactly sure, you can research it online Chelsea." He saw even as he answered she was staring and typing on her phone. "I know people get paid a smaller amount as an option on a book, a kind of holding fee while someone tries to see if they can get it made as a movie. "I don't care how much they paid for the rights, if I was the author I'd want to kill whoever made all kinds of changes to my book!" exclaimed Roddy Gray, with Alfie (his custom life size male doll companion) nodding in agreement   Mrs. Darknight made another rare comment in her gloom laden voice,"I imagine if the director makes changes or a bad job filming Mr. Radcliffes screen play, his life might be in peril.

I've read that it imperative for Mr. Radcliffes career this movie succeed."

Everyone was surprised, that of all people, that the distant, and usually bleak, Mrs. Darknight was aware of the stars career or movies at all. She answered their looks of astonishment, saying, "There was an over looked TV mini series of Wuthering Heights years ago, where Cal Radcliffe played Hinton, Catherines monstrous brother. I thought he was delicious. Critics are fools." She sniffed. Many present were marveling to think this generally depressing woman, might have hidden romantic depths to her dark moody nature, *Very Bronte.*

"Well, I hope to see some of you as extras over the next few weeks," Jack said. "But be prepared for early call time and long days."

Jack sat down next to Mike ending his talk.

The room scattered into movements of drinking, chatting about what the coming weeks of movie making might be like.

Chapter 5 - Holding

A week later, a number of the book group were cast as extras for the film, even Roddy Grey's doll boyfriend. (The directer thought it would be fun to have him in the back of the courtroom gallery — especially as an *unpaid* extra)

All the bookclub members met up and sat together in the holding tent.

Holding - was where the background actors or extras waited, and waited and waited — until they were needed on the set.

Justin realized Holding was like purgatory...a

kind of limbo... In holding you waited not knowing what was coming next, or when... Your job was just to be ready.

It was a good thing Justin was a morning person. Every almost movie day started very early. (Although there were also was the possibility all night shoots...)There was a *process* in the morning, daily *rituals* of checking in with production assistants or PAs, to get marked off as being there, and to be given your work voucher, which you filled out at the end of the day to get paid.   After checking in, you then waited till you got called for the wardrobe line, where you would be looked at for what you might have brought to wear, or to be given wardrobe. Then you went to the make up line, then the hair line. After going through all the proper preparation stations, eventually there was a final lineup where everyone was to be checked over, and adjustments made if needed...

Then you *might possibly* get selected for groupings or *beginning placement* in a scene...All this, usually well before six AM.

Some of the PAs, jokingly called the extras: background artists.

There were about sixty people in the tent in the parking lot, outside the church hall where the courtroom set was. Also there was another place, referred to as satellite holding close to set... actually in the church.

There was a lively atmosphere in the holding tent...with everyone finding their places at the tables and chairs, staking their claims, setting down their garment bags, wheelie suitcases, unpacking their laptops or books...

Justin's fellow non-bookclub extras were generally a friendly group, helpfully sharing information in the confusion...

There was a group of about ten veteran extras, who had come up from downstate. They sat at two of the many tables, clubbed together. Knowing the drill, they set up quickly in the well honed routine of movie veterans.

The majority of people were local newbies, who had brought too much or too little and fluttered around before settling...But they all were excited about being in a movie. And they were all happy to be getting paid to be in a movie, to be professional.

Chelsea showed up a bit late and took the seat Justin had saved for her. She was more interested in observing as a writer, then acting... She said she was being embedded in this showbiz war-zone. Her eyes took in everything, there was so much to see. The activity was so frenetic, everyone doing something, or many things.

You need to be young to be for this, you really need stamina, she thought. But she realized that there were many older folks there.

Chelsea, noticed one particular sweet looking elderly woman. She wished her aunts were here, they would enjoy how much she looked a perfect Miss Marple with her tight bun of blue silver hair and her high lace collar...and her hat with the red silk flower. Something was maybe a little odd about her. Her shoes maybe, she thought, or was it she looked to perfectly Miss Marple? But then, there were so many odd characters moving to and fro all around; chattering with each other, getting their work vouchers passed to them, filling them out, asking questions about filling them out and if they had the right ID. It was all so much to learn.

Also wardrobe and the hair and make up people finished their set up at their tables with mirrors along one end of the tent. They began calling for people to line up for hair and make up...

Chelsea wasn't all that excited about getting to be part of a movie the way Justin and some other Nottinghill Lane folks were. But she did find it allowed her to be behind the scenes in a way that was fascinating. There were so many diverse characters in the holding tent, for the junior reporter to study and observe, the make up and wardrobe people as well as the other extras.

She shared her thoughts with Justin as they sat side by side on folding chairs at one of the long tables in the tent. They had managed to get a spot at a front table just past where make up was set up, but with their backs to the tent wall, so they were out of the way, but with a perfect vantage point to watch all the action in the room, which ebbed and flowed but remained constantly buzzing.

"Justin it's kind of like being embedded in a war zone don't you think? Like what you read about war zones, with planing the shoots like a campaign, readying the background troops for the siege of the courtroom scenes."

Justin chuckled agreeing with her comparison, "We're all waiting for our make up camouflage, our wardrobe uniforms and the command from the PA to march to the battleground of the set. It is pretty crazy."

Chelsea nodded and made furious notes on her iPad. "It sure is."

A friendly deep voice from the next table to the

right piped in, "You think this is bad, you should have seen what it was like before people brought their computers and phones to work and play on," said a round figured, silver haired man. He wore a brown suit, looking like a proposers stockbroker or banker. "Years ago people brought books and magazines, but there was a lot more chatter."

"More than this?" Chelsea's eyes widened in disbelief. "I guess you've done this a lot before?"

He introduced himself, "Bart Hartman, I am an actor at the Fielding Play House downstate in Ann Arbor. But that is seasonal, so I do what ever comes up; voice over, commercials, and background like this. We don't get that many major motion pictures here, so we all trouped up." He gestured to the others at his table, men and women from looking to be anywhere from their 20's to 70. Chelsea wasn't sure age wise. But they all glanced her way and smiled or waved.

"You all came together?" Justin asked, "You

mean like theatrical gypsies?"

Bart and his friends laughed and nodded, "Exactly like the actors did in Shakespeare's day, it's a proud tradition."

"Maybe not so proud," a red haired girl said.

"Well, traditional anyway," said Bart jovially. "Most of us have some kind of other jobs, but none of us wanted to miss the chance of working on this. It's these kinds of films where you have the best chance of getting an upgrade, when there's not a lot of local talent to cast from."

"I'm local talent," Justin quipped.

"You are?" Chelsea said, "I mean, of course you are local and ...talented. But are you an actor?"

"I am now," he said proudly.

"That's the spirit my boy! However, what I mean is, in New York or LA they can just call hundreds of casting agents and hire people with long resumes. Whereas up here in the wilds of Northern Michigan your odds of getting tossed a line or two are much better. That includes you, maybe you'll be lucky...." He looked at them for names.

"Hi, I'm Justin, and this is…"

"Chelsea…but I am not aspiring to act, I'm a writer."

"Good for you! I noticed your rapid fire typing, a screen play? With perhaps with a part for a dashing older gentleman?"

She grinned, "Well, I was just making notes about all this for an article or a story," she gestured to the bustling room. "But now that you mention it, a screen play might be interesting. Our local book group recently had a discussion about the books becoming screenplays and it became quite heated."

"Really? Why was that?" Many faces at both tables looked at her with interest, especially as a number of her book group friends had found places at her table.

"Well, it seems that there often isn't much left in the script from the original books."

Bart and friends nodded and murmured, "That's the way Hollywood, or the business seems to be. They option something, then hire many writers to improve it to the taste and ideas of the executives, producers and stars..."

"Why do they waste money buying it in the first place? Why not just write an original script from the start?" Justin enquired.

"Often they do, but even original screenplays get changed a lot," The veteran actor explained. "I heard this was actually written by the star Cal Radcliffe, or at least his name is on it."

Out of the corner of her eye Chelsea noticed the quaint little old lady she had admired had quietly slipped away at some point. Maybe she wasn't part of this group of actors from down state and she wanted a quieter corner.

Bart beamed brightly, "Justin, you have asked the million dollar question, to which I have no answer. I know they also buy lots of treatments, just 10 pages or so that outline a story, plot and characters... Changing the subject to another important one, have you seen Craft service?"

The two newbies look baffled.

"Food and coffee," Bart explained, " it's a table set up where the snacks are. Also it is the central place for mingling and gossiping. Let's go scope it out."

And away they went as a little group.

Later in the week when Chelsea and Justin were getting used to the crazy routine of *hurry up and wait* of the movie set, they began to understand why the craft service snack table was so important. It was a combination reward center and information and conversation place as background actors ebbed and flowed, getting drinks and snacks and looking to see if any new offerings had been put out on the table. Or if any one had heard updates of breaks or next scenes to be shot.

Chelsea typed into her phone notes, "In the long waiting periods on a film, the boredom causes a strange shift in the importance of food. And a table filled coffee and drinks, with baskets of fruit, little bags of chips, and cookies ... seems like an oasis in the desert of waiting. The sudden appearance of any new plate of veggies and dip, or little sandwiches can cause a flurry of huddling extras like a gaggle of geese pecking for food."

As the crowd broke into small chatting groups after the plates were quickly emptied, Chelsea's ears pricked up for any colorful conversation.

It was then, she heard the first whispers of the films possible phantom...who was causing odd things to happen around the movie set.

Chelsea, who had grown up modeling herself on Harriet the Spy (from the wonderful book) listened intently hoping she could get more information about what sounded like an intriguing mystery.

"I've seen the phantom, all dressed in black," a young girl with the jumble of bright blonde curls said, sounding rather boastful. She was costumed in a demure lavender suit.

"I'm sure that's what wardrobe put her in that

outfit," Justin whispered in an aside to Chelsea, "I think I saw her come in this morning in cut off jeans and a halter top, not so appropriate for a courtroom stenographer."

Chelsea asked, she tried to sound casually curious, "When was that? What did he look like?"

The girl seemed to like that she'd gotten peoples attention, she responded,"Remember the day that the director got so ill, with food poisoning...and Cal and Jessica took turns directing each other."

Justin said, "Yes, and they both did so well. It looked like it really perked Jessica up."

"Well," the blonde continued, "I saw this figure, a guy I think. Dressed all in all black, jeans, sweatshirt, sneakers. That's why I noticed, I couldn't decide if it was a cool fashion look or not...Actually, I couldn't really tell if it was a guy or not. Also, I wasn't sure if he was crew, catering, or what. I mean it didn't look like wardrobe for the courtroom scene, but he-it, could have been for another scene... Anyway he was only around for a few seconds, zipped in, seemed like he maybe put something in directors Barker's coffee. I mean it was fast, and it was dark. Then they were shooting and I was peering from the off camera waiting for the turnaround when they'd need me in the shot at the stenograph machine near the judge...."

Someone else spoke up, a young local guy dressed in a grey suit, one of the other courtroom spectators, "I saw him too. I thought it-he looked odd, and I don't know why, but I followed him... This shadowy looking guy streaked silently through the dark halls, back where the judges chambers are supposed to be. I used to be in the choir in this church, and I kinda know my way around back there, the robing room and stuff. That's where they have it set up for the stars to sit. And this phantom guy disappeared right at the top of a little set of stairs near where Jessica's temporary dressing room is."

"Maybe it was a ghost," someone listening

said, an older man dressed like a lawyer. Who then took a big bite of a bagel with cream cheese, one of the snacks that had just been set out.

"Or someone wanting to pretend to be a ghost," Justin said, as he also grabbed a fresh bagel.

Chelsea out of the corner of her eyes looked at the man who had said ghost... Noting there was something familiar about his face. Also he looked fake old, his silver hair was a wig, not too obvious, a good one, but she could tell, as was his mustache. He was made up, which on a movie was normal enough, but she didn't think she'd observed him in the make up chairs that morning, granted she could have missed him. But there was something about him that tickled her mind a bit. Maybe it was his shoes, brown wingtips that didn't go with the gray suit. She snuck her phone out of her pocket to sneak a picture of him. When she glanced up he was gone.

The blonde girl turned her nose up at the carbohydrate filled bagels, reached for a sparkling water and added to her story, "Well, if you remember, that afternoon the director did get a bit sick suddenly. Luckily the director didn't die, he just was confined to the bathroom for the day...so it could have been food poisoning."

Justin whispered to Chelsea, "I'm sure Mike will want to hear about this. But better just keep it quiet for now. But if it what was someone trying to get to Jessica Zane too...."

"Unless," Chelsea wondered, "what if...?" She faltered as her mind tried to puzzle the different possibilities.

Justin asked,"What if what?"

"Where was her assistant? What's her name? Whitney?"

"Why would she want to make the director sick or cause trouble?" Justin asked.

"I'm not sure. She just seems to always be posing up everywhere." Chelsea said, "Maybe something happened to her or Miss Zane on another film, and she has a grudge," she speculated.

"She does seem awfully loyal to Jessica," Justin said.

Chelsea had thought a bit more, "But this film is important to her, so maybe I'm being silly."

"Maybe?" Justin laughed.

Chapter 6 - Willing Prisoner

Mike: I wasn't surprised that Jack was surprised, when I told him I had agreed to be, not just a consultant on small town policing on the film, but also secretly, extra security for Cal Radcliffe. Apparently some bad things went on during his last film, he want to be cautious on this one. Already there have been a few odd pranks.

Jack had warned me about the movie's star, so I knew that Cal was a hound dog when it came to young men. I am hoping to keep him on a leash, and walk him away from his worst instincts. Just from my first brief introduction it's pretty obvious he would like to handle my gun and fondle my bullets... Cal Radcliffe's as subtle as a car alarm.

But I wasn't worried, I could handle him, and there were reasons working closer, could actually be helpful; I could make sure he kept a polite distance from Jack, I could investigate at close hand any clues, or suspicious activity that could signal another attack or attempt on Cal's life. But also, as I explained to Jack, I kind of feel sorry for the guy.

I know he's a movie star, but especially after all Jack's told me about the movie business, which now isn't such a glamorous thing to me. I think I'm good at reading people, you have to be in my profession. It seems to me Cal is pretty damaged goods. He plays himself in life, a confident cocky celebrity with a sardonic humorous charm. He does it well, that's his profession. But to me the signs of his inner loneliness and insecurity are pretty plain underneath.

For one thing Cal is the kind of person who can't be alone, he needs someone to be reacting to him or he's deflated and is left with only his personal demons.

Lucky for Cal, his assistant Duane seems to be quite a masochist, who needs to be feeling like he's a slave and being punished at the same time. But maybe is just doing what underlings do to get ahead in Hollywood. It doesn't mean he might not have resentment boiling under his nerdy surface.

Anyway, I thought being around, up close on the production would hopefully be safer for everyone, especially my Jack.

I've requested the LA files on the dead body found on Cal's last movie. A cop friend of Jack's in LA told him he'd heard there was something odd about it, hopefully it's in the report.

As far as danger on this set, there's only been a few close calls so far. Which I'm told can happen on any set, who knew what a dangerous business this is?

Cal and his director have asked me to keep quiet about my role as security, for the sake of the production I am just a consultant detective. Accidents happen on sets, Chelsea showed me a list of fatalities in the making of various films. For now, I'm keeping a watchful eye and tight lips... but we'll see.

Jack, thinks I'm a bit crazy. I can tell, he's worried for me. But he's trying not to say anything, which I love him for.

* * *

Cal's personal assistant Duane felt he was servant to a king, he was a fan of history. In his mind he was part of a royal court and Cal was his royal master. He knew there had been a valued member of royal medieval British courts: the Master of the Stool, who ministered to the king in his water closet and aided him in going to the toilet! As odd as it sounds, it was an enviable and coveted role as it allowed the Lord (usually a high ranking nobleman) private time with the king to ask favors for various people. He was payed many bribes to put forward peoples requests. This was how Duane saw himself as he sat outside Cal's open bathroom door on a daily basis. He talked and listened, mostly listened, to his movie star masters thoughts, and orders, reviewed his schedule or ran lines with him. Cal hated to be alone for a moment.

If there happened to still be a young man in Cal's suite leftover from the night before, it was part of Dune's job to either make him disappear or schedule his return, depending on the circumstances. Watching the nudity and sexuality in this process was part of the voyeuristic extras in his personal assistant work. It was a perk he silently savored.

Duane had a special chart he kept on his bosses "dates" with columns for rating the young mens pluses and minuses. Playing this rating game was often a large portion of their daily conversation. He had a similar chart for men his boss as yet wanted to score with.

Both Jack and Mike were on this chart....

* * *

Unknown to the star and secretary, often outside the star's bathroom windows frosted glass, a black hooded figure crouched on the hotel fire escape. Listening...taking notes. Biding his time.

* * *

Jack: I didn't tell Mike that I had a little encounter with Cal. Mike was off at the police station checking in, when Cal asked if I would come to his trailer run over one of our scenes. I knew something was up, because I don't have a lot of lines in any of my scenes, some of my few lines are important, but brief. But I was curious to see Cal Radcliffe one on one...he is a great actor and a big star...I was also curious if that was really what he wanted. Of course, I was not surprised when Cal tried to playfully make a play for me.

I playfully pretend he was kidding. I almost felt guilty about the look on his face when I laughed, but then he laughed too and we both played it like a flirtatious joke.

I managed to gracefully retreat, my zipper intact.

But nothing happened, Mike doesn't need to know. Though he might suspect...

* * *

Justin: Jack had warned to be carful around Cal. But sometimes when someone tells you not to eat candy, it's all you want to do. Whenever would I again get to be in this close to a movie star? To me he wasn't just Cal Radcliffe, he was Captain Blaine Of Starship Explorer, he was Ned

Cutlass the Pirate King, Danny Seldono the mob fixer and Ramsey Dunn the time traveler.

Yes, he was kind of old and kind of puffy in real life, but on camera with the make up and lighting, focused in on his character, he sparked.

Having someone like him paying attention to me was super flattering. He's rich, he's famous and he has zillions off fans and he wants to spend time with me. He says I have an interesting mind, especially for such a young guy.

Ok, I'm not stupid, he doesn't need to take my clothes off to see my mind. But when it's happening, it's like I'm in a movie, his face is close and his breath is hot, I'm seeing him like he's on the big screen...I'm kind of watching him and me on this couch as if it's part of a film. He's the star and has this power, I have to do what he wants. Images of seduction scenes in film flicker across my brain as his hands unbutton my shirt. Sweet young things with millionaires, kings, outlaws, movie stars...allowing themselves to be taken, then comes love, fame, wealth, power...in the movies...

There is a haze of unreality in the room, is this really happening to me I wonder, as my clothes slip off, as his clothes come off. I have more to drink on top of my already tipsy state. Cal's body is far from buff, without the movie lighting and make up he's not handsome, but his eyes are grey ice freezing me and fascinating. I'm like a mouse hypnotized by a cobra...I want this celebrity to want be, to become part of his stardom by intimacy... but something feels wrong. As his hands rub me, begins to make me helpless...I pull back. This is no dream, this is really happening.

What did I do? What would I have done?

Thank goodness there was a knocking at the door and Chelsea's voice was calling out for me, "Justin, come on, your parents are wondering where you are. Come on we have to go now! "

Cal's slightly panicked voice whispered, "How old are you?"

"Eighteen, but I still live at home," I answered as I was quickly pulling my clothes back on, all backward, inside out and mis-buttoned. I could see how relived he was that I was legal. There was a rushed mix of expressions on his face as I moved to the door, I couldn't read them all; disappointment, hunger, anger, challenge...Was I escaping a vampire who wanted to suck my youth, or a hunter who wanted my unicorn head on his trophy wall? Was he just a lonely man who didn't want to be alone? Or all of them?

Safely in the car with Chelsea clucking at me like a scolding mother hen, I felt both like I'd escaped and like I'd missed my chance, but I nonetheless I had an experience.

Chelsea: Poor Justin, he's been in unrequited love with Hank for ages. And all his other crushes are one way too. It's made him very insecure. I'm sure that's why he was vulnerable to Cal Radcliffe, one of the reasons anyway.

Good thing I grew up with Harriet the Spy as a

role model, so I had my eye on his situation and could come to his rescue. Hopefully in a way the movie star will be miffed at me, not Justin.

Justin is so sweet, and he is cute in his nerdy Peter Pan way, I think it's because he doesn't think he's cute, that he doesn't get better response from boys. And that he's grown up on books and fantasy so he's usually walking on some cloud, which when he stumbles off of into reality he gets bruised.

Good thing he has me as a friend.

Another local background guy had a story to tell...Chelsea and Justin listened with astonished ears...

Joe: When I got a chance to be an extra on this movie I was hoping to see Cal Radcliffe, I love his movies. But I never thought I'd sleep with him.

It was just once. And I don't remover it all clearly, I was kinda drunk, I don't remember was that the sex was all that great or anything...but still, I slept with a movie star, Captain Blane -

Galaxy explorer! My friend Pete told me he did too. I guess conquering galaxies makes you lonely and horny.

* * *

Cal Radcliffe thought to himself he wasn't purely selfish, he had over time, helped many of his casual young men in their lives and careers. He tried to help them all, at least to make them feel like they'd had the gift of a moment with a movie star... He didn't just take, it was an ego boost for a nobody to have been with a movie star, Oscar winner Cal Radcliffe.

Cal finished tossing himself off, cleaned up tied his robe and lay back on his bed, lounging as he poured himself another drink, took hit off his vaporizer.

He'd had this background extra Joe, local Joe, who was mid-western hot, corn silk hair, sky blue eyes and a rowers body...he was fun. If the kid ever made it out to LA he'd keep his word and introduce him to some producers and stars. He had a circle who passed each other new young treats. Some guys even ended up in relationships. He never had.

Cal always wanted what was just out of reach. He always had.

He thought about the young guy Justin who had been virtually snatched from his arms by that red headed girl knocking on his trailer and dragging him off... Too bad he'd miss out having him, Justin so young and fresh, and worshipful.

The movie star loved the young men's eyes as he tried it on with them, the amazed, thrilled looks in their eyes, like he was a dream coming true. Sometimes they told him which of his roles, which character they were picturing him as when he kissed them. Other times he tried to guess from the look in their eyes. It made it easier for him to slip into acting a part as he seduced. It made sex more fun to doing things that character might. When it was just him playing movie star, well that was a role too.

When had he last been himself having sex? Maybe there was no such thing,

When had he first been himself with another man, that had been acting too, he didn't know what his scoutmaster was doing, at first, then Cal eagerly acted like he was earning a new merit badge.

* * *

When Duane's phone vibrated he blinked the sleep out of his eyes, read the text, then he got up from his bed and left his room to go next door to sleep on the couch in a Cal's room. Cal couldn't be alone. Duane knew it was one of those empty bed nights, who ever he'd been with had left. Tonight the star couldn't use drink or pills to ease his demons, he had to be Cal need to be as rested and sharp as he could be for shooting in the morning. It was part of Duane's odd job to be the nighttime body guard and keep Cal's nightmares at bay.

* * *

Outside in the dark, mysterious eyes watched the window of the movie stars room as the curtains closed and the lights went out.

Chapter 7 - Professional Users

The movie had been shooting for a two weeks. Things had been going well, as the various courtroom scenes were filmed establishing the intriguing opening of the film. Also there had been some dramatic moments from the climax of the film as they returned to the court room for the ending.

During one witnesses dramatic testimony

news reporters and photographers rushed to the front of the audience gallery area overly enthusiastically, some aggressive extras wanting to close to the camera and be seen, it caused people to be bumped and knocked in the mayhem. The Production Assistants scolded and wrangled the rowdy extras. But it was unsettling too many of the locals who were new to the business. The films director, thought it worked in the camera so let it pass.

* * *

On the Saturday day off, Justin was visiting Jack and Mike in their carriage house studio, wanting to talk about the filming and hoping to see handsome Hank. Maybe gardening with his shirt off. His friend Greer who was hot in a darker way, he was curious to see more of. He couldn't decide whether to be jealous or lustful. Greer was quiet and watchful, like a Labrador dog, always near Hank, always being helpful in whatever digging, building or planting he needed help with. But too close for Justin's comfort.

As Jack sat with Justin on the sofa in the living room they watched the industrious activity of the two young men in the garden outside of the open French doors. They were doing the initial steps for the new garden plots.

Jack and Justin settled comfortably in to their admiring distance, both of them happy to watch, tried from the days of film work. Jack could tell his young friend had a need to voice his new experiences.

"Wow, the movies are dangerous..." Justin said to Jack as he sipped his lavender ice tea, Mike's latest drink experiment, a successful one.

Jack looked at him questioningly, "I don't disagree, but what specifically are you talking about?"

"Well, I was in the courtroom scene yesterday morning and there was a point when they directed all the reporters to rush up to the front of the seats to the gate, and they were crazed, like a herd of buffalo, all wanting to be in front and get their faces in the shot."

Jack sighed, "Gee, I was hoping people around here would be more calm than in LA."

"I don't think these guys are local, there are a lot of the background people that drove up from down state. Chelsea and I met a nice groups of them. But there are others..." Justin said,"some of them are like gangs."

"That's not surprising, this is a very gypsy business, at every level." Jack sighed.

"How did you deal with it?" Justin asked.

"Well, I was just lucky, mostly... And had some good advise from some good people."

Justin rolled his eyes, and told him about what he'd read about Alfred Hitchcock's filming the Birds filming...so dangerous.

They chatted and gossiped and shared their trailer moments with Cal Radcliffe, swearing each other to secrecy. They also talked about the possible phantom on the set.

* * *

After Justin, Hank and Greer all went home, Jack strolled out in to the studio's garden. The unusually warm spring night warped around him like a black silk robe. He watched the lightning bugs flittering and glowing under the stars, it was quietly magical.

He had been up so early he had left his lover sleeping, now at the end of the day he felt the absence of his partner Mike, who was on duty still on set. Jack tried to clear his thoughts and practice mindfulness, a little meditation to center himself, so necessary, especially since he was caught up in the unsettling world of this film. A project he'd thought would only be a few days, now it had stretched into weeks. Not only that, but it seemed he and Mike might become embroiled in yet another odd mystery...or mysterious happenings at any rate.

Sitting in a chair on the patio, Jack was able to close his eyes, let the soft drone of the crickets and evening breeze lull him to peacefully empty his mind and float in the comfortable void... but after a time, images of Mike's handsome face crept in, then his desirable body. The warm feelings that were summoned with the images made him release his meditation and move on to happily meditating on his man and the good luck he'd had in finding him, and the happiness he'd experienced since they'd been together.

He thought about how he loved being with the tallness of Mike...Jack was only slightly below average height at five foot eight inches, but his head came just to Mike's shoulder, the perfect level to rest it on. Being with a taller man, and admittedly a stronger one, did give him feelings of safety and comfort. Which was a candy coating on the miraculous connection they shared with his enjoyment of Mike's sense of humor, his intelligence, his lively curiosity, along with a collection of other quirky and wonderful traits and values...It wasn't just being intimate with a tall strong man that was so amazing...it was this particular tall handsome wonderful man... Jack found himself smiling just thinking about his guy, about Mike's unique specialness.

Images wafted into his mind of some of their loving sensual moments and he felt this meditation on love being distracted by a stirring physical response.

Just at that moment, he heard the door behind him open and arms encircling his neck...

Startled, Jack jumped in his chair.

"Hey it's only me," Mike's warm deep voice said,"Sorry, I didn't mean to startle you." As Jack tilted his head to look up at his lover, Mike leaned down and kissed Jack's lips.

"I was just thinking of you," Jack murmured delightedly.

"Something nice I hope."

"Mmmm, very nice, I was wishing you were here, and here you are."

Mike smiled as he noticed a rise in his partners

trousers, "What other wishes can I grant you oh master? Your genie awaits your command."

"Well, I wish we could share a little wine, and then you might make my magic carpet fly..."

Mike chuckled as he went to fetch the wine and glasses, "Would like me to make your carpet fly up to the bedroom? Or right on the living room rug? Or perhaps Aladdin would like to fly with his genie right here on the grass in the garden?"

"I have to choose only one? Is my genie growing old?"

"Your genie is exhausted from crazy movie people, but could rise to your multiple wishes. Although out here, we might blow out the glow of these lightning bugs with the high voltage of our passion."

Jack stood and accepted his wine glass from Mike, raised it to toast him saying, "Here's to shocking the lighting bugs!"

* * *

Jessica opened her eyes in the darkness of her room, she knew she wasn't home, not in LA or New York... She lay still as gradually it came into her mind what movie she was working on, and where it was shooting—Michigan, that's right...a sweet little town...a safe little town...Bluewater.

Suddenly her eyes flashed wide in fright!

But there was a crazed stalker out there somewhere!

She quickly felt for the switch of the bedside lamp, turning on the soft warm light.

Wait, that stalker was in the movie, the murders were in the script, not in reality.

She sighed, then caught her breath as she remembered outside of the film in reality, there really had been a dead body and death threats on Cal Radcliffes pervious film...

Jessica hadn't been in that movie, it had been a years ago...Why was it in her dreams now? Was she having some sort of premonitions?

Or was bad luck just following Cal. Or was it a

bad person following him...a stalker?

Some odd things had been happening around this movies set, maybe not to her, not yet. But she felt there was an atmosphere of danger.

She sat up, her head felt fuzzy from the whiskey night cap she'd drunk.
There was still whiskey in the tumbler beside her bed, she gratefully took a few deep sips.

No, she hadn't blacked out, the alcohol had just put her fast asleep. Her black outs were from drinking too much to ease her nerve disorder... The tremors had been under control but stress exacerbated them... Did she do things she didn't remember in a black out? She knew she did, but not what, just that she'd sometimes suddenly find herself somewhere else. Was it like sleepwalking?

You couldn't harm yourself when you were blacked out... no that was being hypnotized. Or was it sleep walking. Certainly people had accidents sleep walking.

Jessica poured herself a small shot of whisky.

She had awakened at a table in restaurant and not known how she got there. Jess wondered could she have murdered someone when she was blacked out and not know she'd done it?

Am I really losing it like poor Marilyn? Jessica identified with Marilyn Monroe, who, though a movie star and successful, still felt an emptiness inside, that she hoped being famous and adored would fill...

Now that Jessica knew full well that the reality behind the glamour of movie stardom is hard work, and a massive amount of pretending on and off screen...She felt as she thought Marilyn must have, stardom isn't the dream or solution to insecurity she hoped. At times it's wonderful, at times, it's tedious, sometimes magical, sometimes time scary.

As the sleepy actress sipped her tumbler of comforting whisky she melts into a bleak mood, as memories of things she did to climb to stardom waft in her mind.

If she is honest with herself, Jessica admits, sometimes she amuses herself with the idea of murder! Certainly there are producers she would love to murder, and directors, and male film stars, and female ones too for that matter. There are a large number of people from her past she would like to drop dead.

Jessica's head is filled with script plots and devious of ways to murder people that have done her wrong or annoyed her.

Movie sets can be so tense and tiresome, she is sure that on particularly bad days-sometimes even a production assistant who has been ticked off for bringing a star the wrong kind of coffee might pass the time thinking of ways to murder.

It would be so easy on the sets and locations of movies to kill someone. It could easily be made to look totally accidental. Jessica herself has been asked to do lots of stunts and even simple things can go wrong, horribly wrong; a funny fall that misses the mark and the matt... crack goes your head! That actually had happened to her friend Diane Fremont on the filming of Newspaper Lives.

Jessica has long known making movies can be very dangerous. But for there to be actual murderous intent, that she hadn't experienced before, that she knew of anyway.

Oh dear, these thoughts were not good, it was going to make this a long sleepless night.

Was there more whiskey she wondered.

A soft voice from the other side of the room whispered, "Yes, let me poor you another drink."

Just as she was about to scream, she realized who it was in the shadows of the window seat. Her assistant Whitney, of course it was her. She must have been sleeping on the large cushioned window-seat tucked in the bay window.

"You didn't think I'd not watch over you did you? I know the signs, when you're on the edge." The calm voice said. The young woman came close and sat on the edge of the bed handing her a green capsule, "Here, take this CBD pill, it's only a small dose, but it will help you sleep better than another drink."

"Can I finish this one?"

"Of course. Just remember Jessica, I'm here. I'm always here for you, I hope you know that by now..."

Jessica looked though Whitney's tousled bangs at the girls sweet concerned face, a face now so familiar her.

Jessica realized her young assistant was looking at her with warm dreamy eyes. Loving eyes, that seemed to see her as someone to love despite her afflictions and flaws...

Whitney knew her too well to see her as a movie star...she saw a vulnerable woman.

Suddenly and passionately Jessica wanted the long overdue kiss that was moving towards her, such a gentle, tender kiss.

Chapter 8 - The Hooded Phantom

Everything was going well with shooting that day. The lighting in the barroom of the hotel where they were shooting looked atmospheric and flattering, making both stars - Cal and Jessica look subtly dazzling, as they sat chatting at the end of the bar, patiently enduring the final ministrations of the hair, make-up and wardrobe people.

The work of the entire production team was masterful...There was a positive flow to the mood in the room as the wide master shot of the whole bar room was done quickly, and other cover shots were moving smooth and fast...

Jessica's close ups were emotionally moving as she explained why she had broken up with Cal's character long ago. Cal stood off to the side feeding her his cue lines and reactions. The director and crew applauded her softly after the last sensitive take.

Then, when it was Cal's turn for close ups, his responses were equally real as he reacted with his never dimmed hope, that her character might one day love him again....

Suddenly - CRASH! SMASH! GLASS SHATTERING! SCREAMS.

A huge mirror over the bar came away from the wall falling right toward Cal and the bar, smashing just inches from him.

Or, from where he would have been sitting, had Mike not been close at hand and grabbed him to pull him out of harms way.

Mostly out of harms way.

Cal and others on the crew close by sustained small cuts from flying tiny glass shards, as several bar glasses shattered. But the mirror mostly shattered downward on and behind the bar, contained by the huge ornate frame that had a wood backing.

Mike and Cal had ended up tumbled on the floor. Mike on his back with Cal's weight on top of him. The star had some tiny droplets of blood spotting his face from tiny cuts...Cal's breathing was heavy, he was panting as his eyes connected with Mike's. His expression was wide eyed, with what Mike was reading as shock.

Mike himself soon became the shocked one, as several unexpected things happened rapidly; first, Mike felt Cal's surprising hardness against his thigh. Then Cal's eyes cleared from shack glazed to bright and naughty. He thanked Mike with a throaty voice that implied the movie star was grateful for both his swift saving him from harm, and, for the brief sexual thrill the detectives manliness gave him.

Cal's eyes moved from Mike to swiftly roam over the room, he called out, "Every one all right?" Then he looked to the camera operator and DP, "Did you get that Hal?"

"Yes, both camera's," Hal answered. Cal jumped up, and held his hand out to Mike to help him up. As other Assistants and crew were all gathered like a mob of emergency workers, helping them both up off the floor.

Excited as a kid, Cal moved quickly to the video monitors, near the camera, "Can I see playback on that?" A cluster of people gathered behind him to watch as two shots side by side, close and wide, dramatically replayed the accident. Cal and the DP eyed each other like conspirators, grinning.

"That was some luck I was still running," Hal the Director of Photography said.

"Great, we'll use it!" Cal said to the director who was right there grinning too. They had both experienced unexpected moments caught on film during shooting in the past, sometimes really usable ones.

Mike stood back to watch this scene as well, not sure what to think. He saw various people were sitting or standing at the back of the room getting their small wounds tended to. Luckily no one was more than slightly cut or bruised or scratched, which was very lucky.

Mike moved toward the broken mirror to investigate the cause of its fall. But before he got too close, he was cautioned to wait and stand back while a man with a hand held camera panned and zoomed over the glittering wreckage for coverage shots they might use in the movie.

Once Mike was allowed to move close he saw there was something strange, the strong wire that held the mirror hadn't broken. He moved to the nails in the wall behind the bar, something was very odd he thought. On looking closer he discovered it had purposely been boogie trapped to fall. Set up somehow so it could be remotely trigged, he thought.

Mike wasn't sure what to think, was this the work of the phantom sabotaging the film, with Cal and the director were just taking advantage of it?

Or, was it a plot on their part to create a stunt on the set without warning anyone?

It was deadly dangerous either way.

"But if it was just a movie stunt," Mike thought, "if I find out that's the case, then, I'm outta here. They're on their own."

When Mike looked up from his surveying the damage, the room was already empty, everyone had moved outside for lunch.

Just out of the corner of his eye Mike saw something in the dark in one shadowed corner. Just as he focused enough in the dark on dark to make out a figure in a black hooded sweatshirt, it vanished. There one minute and silently, instantly gone the next, melted in to the darkness, in such a way that Mike was almost uncertain he'd seen it. Almost...

* * *

Chelsea the spunky red haired journalist, was determined to get an interview with Cal Radcliffe. She had approached the Public Relations man for the movie who didn't seem to take her very seriously. He gave her a press kit thinking she was just a kid from a local school paper or blog. When she said she heard there had been some accidents on the set, he became abrupt and sent her on her way.

Covertly Chelsea had been making notes on the film set of the court house when she was an extra. She had put to use her observational skills there. Her other talents of listening and chatting she had utilized with the crew she encountered in make up and wardrobe, and with Jake, one of the cute young production assistants who played guard dog to the extras in holding.

From some remarks cute Jake the PA had made about the passes the films star had made at him, Chelsea thought she might have a secret weapon to get her interview with Cal, if, she could charm Hank into acting as her photographer. She was sure once the lusty movie star got an eyeful of that hunky pretty boy, he wouldn't slam his dressing room door on the pair of them. If he had liked Justin, he'd be crazy about Hank.

She had saved Justin from Cal's clutches, and she wasn't going to leave Hank on his own...

She wrestled in her mind about the morality of using a friend in this manner, and in sexually baiting a reporter trap. She managed to rationalize to herself, she wasn't out to get a trashy story about Cal Radcliffe's sexual interests. She just wanted to get a basic interview. Certainly letting him glimpse the eye candy of Hank's good looks, was just that, a treat, like looking at a beautiful Greek statue and that's all he would get, but that was something.

As for Hank, if he could be talked into it, he could feel good that he was doing her a favor, and helping her career as a journalist. He'd be meeting a movie star up close, and he might like that, as long as it wasn't too up close.

She hadn't totally convinced herself she wasn't being dubious. But she'd done a good enough job that she was going to go ahead with her plan, at least to see if it was workable. She could always pull the plug at the last minute. (Chelsea had a feeling these were the famous last words of many disasters)

When Chelsea stopped by the carriage house the next afternoon to share a basket of her Aunts baked treats and her own special ginger iced tea with Hank, she was did her best to be subtle.

She was enthusiastic about Hank's design for the new garden addition, and the early progress. She was nice to his friend Greer, which was easy as he was almost as cute as Hank.

The boys were only too glad to take a break

and savor her offered treats...

Why was Chelsea suddenly feeling like the Big Bad Wolf instead of Red Riding hood?

* * *

Cal Radcliffe often felt like the Big Bad Wolf, except he was afraid, and he was afraid of his fears. He used what ever he could to distract his mind from thinking about them.

Some of his distractions were constructive; acting and producing, getting a movie project or play up and running and out in the world.

Of his other distractions alcohol and sex were his favorites, but both could be addicting...more drinks, more handsome young men, habits.

He was afraid of addiction, so it was a fearful cycle.

Sometimes fear made one do unexpected things, things he regretted, or would, if he ever let himself think about them.

Chapter 9 - The First Body

It was cold by the lake in the morning, especially on out on the out crop of land at the edge of the park bordering the harbor. The cold was a contrast to the hot lights from the weeks of indoor filming. Some of the crew were figuring out how to corral the ducks and geese that were wandering the shore for food. They were a potential noise issue for the soundtrack. The location was only in the very first stages of being set up, as the near by parking lot was beginning to fill with cars and vans of the crew at the crack of 5AM. The sun was still waking up, just beginning to part the horizon in the East, while stars were still dimming in the West, such is the need for movies to be ready to capture every daylight moment.

* * *

Jessica was not on the call sheet for the day, so she was settled in her hotel suite resting and reading, still rather frazzled by the mishap with the mirror on the set a few days before.

Not that she had been in danger, but she would have been a few minutes earlier. Jess had seen her share of accidents the set over the years, and had some close calls of her own.

An announcement had been made that, the set dresser had not checked the stability of a mirror, as it was part of the existing decor of the hotel bar...and supposedly the vibrations from the movements of camera equipment had been the trigger that caused its wires to snap. Jessica had an uneasy feeling about this incident. Her assistant had informed her there were whispers going round saying maybe it had actually been a stunt the director had secretly organized. Though others were whispering about a phantom.

She sat at the dressing table gazing in the large triple mirror at her own eyes, blue-grey and cool. But, behind her seemingly calm eyes...was fear, despair, and anger. For a second she trembled with momentary panic, as she thought these mirrors trembled. But she realized it was knock at her door. Quickly she composed herself, adjusting her upswept hair as she called out,"Come in."

Her assistant Whitney entered with a vase of white roses; looking rather white and pale herself.

"Whitney is something wrong?" Jessica asked concerned.

"Jess, they found a body on the set this morning," she answered in an uneven tone of voice as she tried to set the flowers carefully on a table by the windows-seat.

"Sit, sit you silly girl. Calm down. There was supposed to be a body by the pier in the park. Remember, they're shooting the discovery of the first murder victim today," Jessica looked at her assistant, struggling to overcome her own nerves. She pasted on a beaming smile as though she was shining a light on a little problem making it dissolve away. Whitney lowered herself on the cushioned window-seat.

Sighing she looked into the beautiful face of the actress, softly she explained, "Yes, but there was a body already there, a real body!"

"An actual dead body?" Jessica wondered, as she turned around from her dressing table to look at Whitney's drawn face. As she echoed the words "dead body" trying to understand, trying to have the impossible sink in.

The assistant rasped, "Yes, a corpse, of a young woman, with a red scarf around her neck like in the script. She even had the gold bird pin on her sweater like the ..." her voice trailed off.

Jessica completed the thought, "...The murder

victims in the film," she gasped, "oh my god. Do they know who...how ?"

The assistant shook her head, "The detective on the film was there, Mike, Officer Page, and he took charge. He's the one that's been shadowing Cal. His boyfriend is Jack the actor playing the young policeman...He was supposed to find the body in the scene they were filming this morning...In the movie he's called to the crime scene, and finds Peter the guy who gets accused of the murder. But early this morning Jack the actor, found a body in reality...already there on the lakeshore."

Jessica was confused, "Wait, he found the body in the movie or this mornings real body?"

"Both, isn't that bizarre?" Her voice was filled with awe and trepidation, "Reality and film sometimes do overlap or collide...unbelievable."

"Do they?" Whitney wondered.

Jessica stood and began to pace nervously, her long silk dressing gown floating behind her.

"This is a plot...it has to be. The strange thefts,

the notes, then the mirror falling, now a body..."

"Notes? What notes?" Wit asked.

"Oh just silly things I've found and throw away, just odd poem fragments...but disturbing to find in unexpectedly tucked in drawers in my dressing room."

"The dead body was it a girl? Like the victims in our script?" Jess asked.

"Yes."

"Was she on our film? Or was she local?"

"I don't know. I didn't see her. She was covered up when I got there."

"You were there? You didn't just hear about it?"

"I only went down to watch for a bit, I wanted to see Jack act. I was a fan when he was young on his TV show. But then..." she started to cry.

Jessica took Wit in her arms, comforting her new lover also helped to comfort herself. Soon they were curled up on the kingsize bed spooned together, nuzzling and dosing.

* * *

Jack and Mike had miraculously arrived home at almost the same time, each having different long challenging days. Mike had stayed with the crime scene and then gone to the police station to report and meet with the force about the mysterious crime. Murder was most unusual in this small town. Finally at home that night, at the end of a long horrific day, where, despite a dead body being discovered on the original shooting location, the director pushed ahead with the scheduled day, just moving the location to the other end of the waterside park.

Mike was shocked at first by the filmmakers — the show must go on attitude — but he came to see, how focusing on the project and the process helped everyone calm down and move on from a situation they could do nothing about once the initial statements and questions had been answered. Everyone was still near by in the park if the police need them.

Since very little equipment had been set up, the crew left it, and just relocated the video village of the monitors for the director and the cameras and the rest farther down the shore away from the taped-off crime area.

It was still early, only six thirty in the morning. Not many people had arrived to set up by then. Easy to more the set up and the crew to another parking lot on the other end of the park.

Jack had been a very early bird that morning. The gruesome discovery was so early, because Jack had trouble sleeping before his first solo scene, and knowing he had to be on location by six am, he decided to bring his coffee and walk downtown to look at the lakeshore park where they would be shooting his scene.

When he found the park bench by the waters edge for the shot they were doing, he noticed a dark shape on the ground on the far side of the bench. He thought is was someones sleeping bag at first. But then seeing it was a person, he thought maybe it was the prop body for his discovery scene in the film. Which was strange that it somehow had been placed there ridiculously early... Certainly if such an expensive prop had been put there, a PA or crew would have been posted to guard it? He was hesitant to look more closely, it looked so real it creeped him out, but he leaned in and saw the girls form was dressed as the script's description. Moments later the dawning sun grew brighter and Jack leaned closer marveling at what an incredible job the special effects people had done on the victim...but then it became all too apparent to him, this dead body was real.

Jack felt a scream pounding inside that wouldn't come out.

With trembling hands he fumbled his phone out of his jacket and had managed to call Mike.

* * *

By afternoon, the body was removed, the crime

scene had been documented, photographed and investigated. One policeman guarded the area sealed off with yellow caution tape.

* * *

Miraculously Jack had managed to film the scene of him discovering the same kind of body, only this time with an actress playing dead. It was very macabre, to be repeating what he had only hours earlier done in reality in was a very bizarre rehearsal...However, it did help to shift his focus, for a time...Jack knew on some level he was having delayed shock. But he had resisted when Mike tried to talk him out of going on with the days filming.

As the day progressed, it became less and less real.

* * *

The day's filming had wrapped by 7pm for Jack. When he found Mike coming in the door just after minutes after him he was surprised. In TV shows you get the impression cops on a murder are wired into the investigation twenty-four / seven. But in reality, and in small towns, things happen at a slower pace. Especially since the doctor who was the corner was not able to examine the corpse until the morning.

Mike had hugged Jack and snuggled with him on the couch, dosing him and himself, with a healthy tumbler of Scotch. He massaged Jack's shoulders and soothed him, coaxing the last bit of stress and shock out of his lover, kissed him, then sent them upstairs for a hot shower before dinner. Though Mike was very tempted to join him, he busied himself with creating a comforting meal, something light as it was late.

Jack looked damp and adorable wrapped in his terrycloth robe as he rejoined his lover, in the kitchen to discuss the very strange day over wine.

Mike explained, "We've even managed to keep it under wraps, which in this town is miraculous."

"How did manage you pull that off?" Jack asked astonished, his blue eyes widening.

"Well, seeing you filming just down aways, people think it's part of the movie, and the Captain said not to say otherwise. Not yet," Mike sipped his wine thoughtfully. As he studied Jack's handsome face, his handsome tired face, Mike was concerned about the dark shadows under his eyes. Jack was having similar thoughts as he looked at his tall, lean lover, who looked more starkly pale, then his usual warm ivory skin tones.

"But you must have had to notify the girls family," Jack said, "oh, I maybe you haven't identified her yet."

Mike had a momentarily thoughtful expression, weighing how just discreet he had to be. But, this was his partner, his lover, his Jack... He refilled the wine glasses, sipping again as he stalled for time...

Then Mike explained, "We have actually managed to identify her. But we haven't alerted the family yet...for several reasons." He sighed and took a breath, "Jack this is going to make this strange situation sound even stranger..."

"How, even stranger?" Jack asked astounded.

"First, because this girl wasn't actually murdered. She committed suicide, overdosed herself on pills. Secondly, because this young woman died four months ago..." Mike's green eyes met Jack's stunned blue ones.

"How is that possible?" Jack gasped. Jack's eyed widened with surprise as he listened to Mike explain... Jack kept staring at Mike waiting to hear more words to make the impossible at all understandable.

"Her body was in storage awaiting burial in a cemetery," Mike explained, "in the winter the ground this far north is too frozen, they have to keep bodies till after spring."

"I didn't know that, I never thought of it..."

Jack said and took a big gulp of wine.

"All I can tell you is what we know so far, or, what we think we know..." Mike said, "She isn't a murder victim, she is actually stolen property."

"Body snatching," Jack whispered.

* * *

Elsewhere in town, the Director James Barker was not sleeping. He was editing footage from the past few days. He would be up all night. He wanted to see how the new scenes would come together. Jack Page had given a good performance. Very real, which under the days very real start, was not a total surprise.

The director was haunted by his failures of the recent years, over ten years since he'd had a box-office hit. Some of his movies had beed good, really good, but just missed. It happened, timing, luck and lots of other things change the fortunes of a movie. Then there had been that terrible accident on Time Warp, with three people killed.

Not his fault. But still the insurance payouts and law suits...the studios were not happy.

Barker needed this movie to work, he needed to astound Hollywood Studios with how he was able to do something amazing on a small budget film. He felt more driven than he ever had on his big budget epics. He smoked his thin vaporizer, and sipped brandy, as he paced back and forth in front of the editing monitors watching the playbacks.

Cal and Jessica both desperately need this film to work, he felt needed it more. He would do whatever it takes to make this movie tense and exciting.

It was almost five in the morning when he abruptly stopped pacing, and wondered: Could I be cracking up and trying to sabotage my own film?

Was there really some phantom out to destroy the this movie? Or someone involved with it?

He knew about the body on Cal Radcliffe's last film, it had been as hushed up as it could be. Just an accident, was the story. A homeless person..they said. But James knew, better.

James sipped his brandy and asked himself: Was any of this phantoms vendetta aimed at me? And, is there a way I could use all this to my advantage?

Barker realized it would soon be close to daylight, he had shower and get ready, the day was going to start very soon.

Chapter 10 - Un-murder

The next morning Mike and the Captain went to see what the coroner could tell them about the unfortunate mystery body.

Dr. Mitch Chambers was a local GP, on call as coroner and medical examiner for several counties, as there was a need to stretch budgets. The Doc was a friendly stocky middle aged fellow with shaggy silver hair and a mustache to match. In his off duty time, Doc liked to ride a motorcycle and walk the wooded acres he was accumulating up in the hills across from the lake.

Detective Mike was on affable acquaintance terms with Mitch. He had met him and his wife socially at local functions. The doctors wife had persuaded Jack to join the local community art center in Bluewater. They were a charming happy couple. But the Doctor was looking very somber this morning, as he greeted the lawmen from the other side of the gurney with the sheet swathed body of the young girl.

"She's been embalmed, that's why she looks as fresh as she does, and she was in cold storage somewhere waiting for the ground to thaw to dig a grave. At least I pretty sure that's the where and why of it. None the less there is a certain odor..."

"I had that much figured out, but it's spring," Mike said,"I would have thought that burials would have been done by now."

Mitch almost chuckled, "Mike, you know better than that. The ground doesn't unfreeze deep down immediately. Even when it does, things get backed, people get backed up...slow to start. Then too, people kinda thaw from winter, have to get back up to speed. Then too, the funeral home would have to schedule when they want to do the burial, if there's to be a ceremony of some kind."

Mike and the Chief both nodded in silent agreement of the logic of this.

"But where would the body have been stored? Would it have been at the funeral home?" the Chief Joe asked.

The Doc shook his head, you know the size of the funeral parlors around here, they can't keep more than a couple of bodies at a time."

"So where then?" Mike asked.

"Well, you may have noticed most cemeteries have out buildings on the property, some of them are used to house bodies in the winter. It's cold enough to keep them there," was the response.

"That doesn't sound too secure," Mike said.

"Well, not many people would know about it, not many people would want to break in if they did," the Doctor said as the folded the sheet down to the girls shoulders, "now, this poor girl, I remember. I had to go to the house and write the report when she was found after she killed herself. It was plainly suicide. She left a heart broken note," Doc Mitch sighed with frustration, "what a waste."

"This is the Peters girl right," Chief Joe asked, "I recall she'd been in some trouble, shop lifting, drugs, boyfriend was a punk dealer...sad. She was a cute kid when she was in my aunts grade school class.

"Which makes me glad she wasn't messed with, she was just moved and dressed in the red sweater with the bird pin and scarf round her neck to mimic a strangling," Mitch said.

"It doesn't seem she could have any connection to the film, or anyone in it." Mike said. "The only local people are extras...Could one person have done this? Broken her out of a coffin and moved her? It would have to be a man wouldn't it?"

The Chief chimed in, "It might have been more than one person, but with the right dolly and lifting skills. Nurses learn how to lift patients. Or maybe just a really fit woman. But why go to all the trouble? Just for a prank? Sick."

"There have been other pranks, or sabotage on the movie," Mike said, "seems someone is trying to damage the film, or someone on the film."

Mitch was gently, respectfully examining the body to see if he'd missed anything as the other two men speculated.

"Who could be hurt if the film shut down, or who has been threatened? Have there been threats?" The Chief asked.

"I'm positive there have been, I suspect both the stars Cal and Jessica may have had threats, but they haven't wanted to say more than that they feel threatened, and the director too. But he's arrogant enough to feel invincible, well as far as his life goes. I think he's worried about the film. But he seems to have blinders on that make him not care about anything but moving forward with the film," Mike explained. "However, I'm certain there is someone who has managed to get on to the sets and in the hotel, someone dangerous. As to what their motive is, I have no clue, not yet."

"It's just weird," Chief Joe said, "I thought having a movie come to town would be fun and good publicity, but now not wanting publicity is exactly why we need to keep this quiet as much as we can."

Mitch snickered, "In this little bee hive? Good luck with that." He looked sheepish, "Of course my lips are sealed."

Mike offered up a thought, "I managed to find out that something happened on Cal Radcliffes last film in LA, which also had the same director. I have to double check, but I think they had a body like this turn up. I need to make certain it was stolen like this was."

"That can't be a coincidence," said the Chief, "but that would mean someone was in LA and is now here."

"Yes, so that possibly gives us some ways to narrow down some suspects from the cast and crew. I still need the LA report on that incident, hopefully there's something in it, some details that could help."

All three men gazed down on the lifeless young woman laid out before them, the murder victim who wasn't murdered.

Most crimes in the semi rural of Northern Michigan were pretty straight forward; car thefts, fights leading to violence, hunting accidents or violations...Puzzling crimes like this didn't come along that often around Bluewater.

All three men in the hospital morgue had minds that didn't like loose ends or unanswered questions, whether medical or criminal.

They all wanted to keep body snatching quiet.

Mike knew he would discuss it with Jack, who was discreet. Jack often helped him look at things differently. Also, he wanted Jack to be aware and cautious on the movie set...To keep his eyes and ears open for any information or observation that might help.

Mike didn't like the idea of his lover or any of

his friends being on the film any longer. But he doubted Jack or the others would quit just because he wanted them too. Especially as Jack was the only one he could tell why, for now anyway. He would tell Justin and Chelsea and the others to keep their eyes open and be careful. The detective needed to find out if any of them had seen or noticed anything, without saying too much.

Mike need to talk to both Cal and Jessica tomorrow, he was certain they both had things that they were withholding from him, and now was the time to get them both to tell.

Chapter 11 - Uninsurable Nightmare

"This crazy, crazy business…" Jessica Zane whispered to herself as she felt the fiery relaxation of her nightly whisky slide down her throat. She was in her hotel suite, which was above and away from production. Which had seemed like a good idea at first, to be close, but not too close, to where she would need to be everyday. She quite enjoyed the faded grandeur of the suite, like an English country house. However she thought to herself more and more often Jess was starting to feel like faded grandeur herself.

She wasn't sure if she was feeling less or less secure in the hotel after all the odd happenings... But hopefully the cute detective Cal had hired had said he was keeping a watchful eye out. And there were some regular security guards watching the equipment and the hotel. She should have told Detective Mike about the weird notes she'd been finding...they weren't threats, but still unnerving.

The actress felt a there was some lurking shadow around...but she wasn't sure. When she'd talked to Cal, he been evasive, oblique in his wording... He said the film was in some trouble because of the few accidents on the set... pranks he called them.

A dead body to her was not a prank, even if it turned out to have been stolen from a morgue and not murdered on the spot...Something the handsome detective had shared with her to keep her a bit calmer.

She was sworn to secrecy, but she was sure it

was already being whispered all through the cast and crew.

How could something so bizarre not be talked about, body stealing! And the body being gothically staged on the movie set. Weirder and weird...Something evil this way comes...Jess thought with a shiver.

In fact Jessica had once been in horror film where there were body thieves, a period horror monster film. She grimaced, it wasn't a terrible film, just kind of cheesy... But she had enjoyed a brief affair with the handsome costar Willam Trent, sadly dead now from cancer. She wasn't that old but already felt mortality around her. Yes, in Hollywood people did shuffle off this mortal coil a higher rate, and often younger. Now death, not just in this films script but actually here on this film set. Sometimes she felt like it was stalking her... still she had to take the risk. She had no other options as good as this might turn out.

Jessica had badly wanted this role. She

thought the film would be a break for her...It was the kind of part that didn't come along often, that would show off her edge and intelligence in a way that could lead to other avenues.

She might become that strong female who could be a lead police inspector of a series, or judge, or power broker in Washington...Those British actress all were able to carry on decades older than she was now. Yes, they had distinctive voices, but she did too. Her throaty rasp had captured audiences and fans in her first big film, the suspense story: Cold Hearts.

The film had been a huge gamble from the start, she knew that going in, Cal had said she might have to put some of her salary in escrow... He claimed both he and the director were going too as well, in order to calm the nervous studio, investors and insurance company...

Cal had sweet talked her, flattering Jessica, insisting that with her tremendous talent (combined with his) the resulting film would be something fresh for them both! It would best of all a hit!

She was overdue for her second Oscar Cal said, he insisted together they would be a winning team, scoring Oscar nominations for both of them! Which fingers crossed, they would win!

Then Cal gave her a steady meaningful look, filled with sensitivity, clinching the pitch by saying, that teammates kept mum about the frailties of each other, as he whispered these words - his eyes lingered on her slightly trembling hand.

He knows, she thought...or does he?

Maybe he just thinks I'm a drunk like everyone else does...

But then again maybe has guessed her real health problems...it was bound to happen sooner or later.

* * *

Jessica paced herself, usually she only allowed herself two drinks of an evening. She was at the end of her first...Listening to Ella Fitzgerald's smooth voice sing: Out of This World...

Cal Radcliffe had been out of this world when he was young, at twenty he was cute in his unique way. While never conventionally handsome, his eyes were so intensely filled with dreams and drive. And he had more hair then, too.

She smiled and sipped her drink as she thought back all those years ago, when she and Cal were young in New York at drama school and waiting tables in the same restaurant.

There was one night, she and Cal had listened to this same Johnny Mercer song late one night after work. Many drinks later, they had made out for a while... and played around some, as you do when you're young. But Jessica knew back then, maybe even before he did, women weren't his thing. But they were young, fresh and giddy with aspiration and possibility. It was long, long before either of them had found fame or bad marriages or career flops. Then Jessica came to realize her slowly creeping illness...it was so unfair, sometime she just wanted to lash out, to punish someone...

Whitney would bring her the second drink soon, and have one too and keep her company. Everyone told her how lucky she was to have such a loyal assistant...a treasure.

Things now had surprisingly developed in a new way, a new love.

Was this love she asked herself? It felt like it. Certainly romances on film shoots were epidemic. But this had grown and developed from her closeness with her young assistant, their friendship.

Jessica thought, "I am just going to enjoy this for now, not question it. I need her, and I want her. And I need her wanting to be with me...So there, nothing more to analyze. At least... not until we get back to LA."

* * *

Morning came with the creeping pain demons riding the actress' bones...Even having Wit in her bed to warm her hadn't prevented her reoccurring pain, their love making may even have exacerbated it. She hoped not.

"I'm going to tell them you're not well. They'll have to shoot around you today. Jess really, you aren't up to it today." Whitney insisted.

Jessica moaned, "No, I have to do this...otherwise they'll think I'm a prima-donna... After the last film..."

"That wasn't your fault."

"No, but it could have been a disaster for me, my body wasn't behaving. I managed to get through the project, barely, not my best performance. I was lucky..." She sighed, how long could she hide her illness? It seemed to come and go, alcohol helped manage the intermittent pain. Yes, everyone in the business thought she had a drinking problem, and she did. But it was really because of her rare strain of arthritis...

In the movie business any illness could make you uninsurable, you'd never be able to work again. Drinking, drugs, were no problem. A stint in rehab and on to a new film. Look at Luke Draper, he turned up naked on someones porch roof last time he fell off the wagon. Now, he had three mega films in a row.

But illness, oh no! An example she always thought of was poor James Dunmore. He was a very cute young actor who'd been a teen idol and was growing into a wonderful young star, when word of his heart murmur got out... and wham out he went. After years teaching he was coming back doing voice over now, thank goodness.

"Up I get Whitney! I can do it. I have to do it. It's what I'm here for, to prove I can." She touched her assistants arm, "With your help I can manage to do it babe." She smiled gratefully and received a light kiss in return. Jessica forced her body up from bed, she knew once she got moving she would grow less stiff and shaky eventually. The CBD salve Whitney had found helped too.

As Wit helped her dress, she said to her, "I'm a damn good actress, with so much I still want to do! I wanted to be one of the rebels who didn't get a facelift and happily play character old grandma's. Maybe one day, I even play a Miss Marple type cozy lady detective."

"Not for decades, silly," Whitney as she went to the door to retrieve the room service breakfast tray. Then she poured them both coffee.

Jessica sipped her much need caffeine and thought, I wonder if I should to try to solve this mystery? Maybe then use turn it into a script? Why not? Maybe as an old dame, my illness wouldn't matter so much...Well, at least it if was my script and my project it wouldn't matter.

She thought she'd just had a brilliant idea. What if her character had her same illness, people win academy awards playing disabilities... like the violinist with MS and the British scientist in the wheelchair. She could certainly plat something a role like that.

***

An ear was pressed to the door of the actresses suite. A person dressed as a maid was listening. The maid had slipped a note onto the coffee tray when the bellman wasn't looking. Now the maid was listening to hear if she finds it. This maid wasn't what she appeared, she was a man in costume, a very convincing one.

The listening man knows Jessica's secret.

He knows lots of secrets.

The listener means Jessica no physical harm, he just wants to throw her off enough, enough to topple the house of cards that is the film...then to revel in the destruction.

The phantom has his reasons, and plenty of tricks up his sleeve. Plenty of disguises like the one he is wearing. He catches sight of himself in the hall mirror. The red wig suits him. The pert black uniform, and stocking. His legs look darn good. He'd have to use this again. This was good rehearsal through. The bell man had given him the eye, which had him worried, until the guy winked at him as he passed down the hall.

Yes, this outfit might be even better for the next surprise than the handyman costume.

What he was going to do was going to be tricker then the body in the park, but he had it all planed. Poor Jessica... but she was a tough lady. You had to be in this dirty business. The movie world had a lot to answer for.

Cal Radcliffe would get his surprise soon too. But he'd been getting surprises all along he wasn't yet aware of. The maid chuckled very softly as she slipped away down the back stairs.

Chapter 12 - Stand Ins

"What, what, what?" Jack laughed with Mike joining in, "You ask more questions in two minutes than anyone I know. You certainly sound like a reporter."

"Or a police detective," Mike said.

"Maybe I'm both," Chelsea said proudly, "they aren't mutually exclusive. Is there more of that yummy lavender ice tea?"

"There is indeed young lady. And perhaps you'd enjoy a super fresh cranberry lemon scone to go with it." Mike offered.

"Super fresh?" Chelsea's eyes glowed delightedly. "Is that what the wonderful baking smell is? Yes, please!"

"You're the junior detective, you should have deduced that Mademoiselle Sherlock," teased Mike as he'd put on his oven mitts and lifted the warm mouth-watering baking tray from the oven, setting it on a cooling rack on the kitchen counter where they all sat.

"I feel like you're bribing me," Chelsea said as a plate with a piping hot scone was set in front of her, along with dishes of butter, thick cream and strawberry jam.

"Well, it might be considered a bribe if you were an actual police person. Or, if you weren't absolutely dying to tell us everything you came here specifically to tell us. But you better quickly eat up the evidence, while it's hot, just in case," Mike teased. And for the next few minutes that's exactly what they all did.

"We better leave some for Justin and Hank and Greer when they get here. Where are those boys anyway, they're late," Chelsea said with her mouth shiny with butter.

"Don't worry, I have another batch I'll pop in when they get here, having the scones hot from the oven is the best part, " Mike said.

"It certainly is," Jack agreed wholeheartedly, humming happily inside that his lover was such a terrific baker.

"Baking and cooking don't always go together," Chelsea stated as if she'd just read Jack's mind. "Take my Aunts for example, Aunt Dot cooks well but her baking is awful, even the birds can't peck her cookies. Aunt Dash isn't a very good cook. But, her cakes and muffins are out-of-this-world delicious!"

Jack and Mike nodded in agreement having enjoyed many treats from the Aunts.

Out of the blue came a new question from the intrepid girl reporter.

"What does a stand-in do on a movie?" Chelsea asked curiously, "They get paid just to stand around? "

Jack had always thought being a stand-in was hard job, and that they should be appreciated... but not all actors felt or acted that way. So he explained to Chelsea how important a stand-ins job was. That having someone stand in an leading actors place allowed lighting to be set up for shots, and blocking to be planed in advance so camera moves could be mapped out and marks could be put in place on the floor or ground so the actors knew where to move to and stand so they synchronized with the lights and camera and other actors. "It saves time, and money not having the stars stand around while everything is being set up."

"Oh I see. But still, are they just standing around? Do they have to look like the star? Enquiring minds want to know," the red haired teenager giggled.

"They don't just stand, they actually have to be very focused, they have pages of the script and have to make notes to remember what they did, to be able to repeat it as needed, and share it with the star if asked." Jack explained patiently, "They have to be about the same height and coloring as the star, but not really resemble them. Though sometimes they will want someone who does, because then they can photo-double."

"What's that?"

"Well, if a shot is the back of their head looking at another actor, or just a tiny bit or far away and indistinct, they can use the double so the star can go..." Jack said, he saw Chelsea's mouth open to ask another question and he anticipated it, "And no, the star isn't being lazy. They may be needed in another shot set up elsewhere, or to change in another costume, or something else."

"Ok, I see, standing in sounds kind of fun," she said.

"Well, yes sometimes, but it's not easy. They have to be in early to the set, way before the star, and stay till the very end of the day, which can be very long. They have to always be watching and ready to step in. And they have to out in the heat or the cold weather too when shooting out of doors. With no trailer to go to like the star might have. But there are people who specialize just in being stand-ins. And there are some stars who insist on their same stand-in all the time. So if the star works a lot, so does the stand-in."

Chelsea got busy making notes about all she'd just heard, murmuring, "Who'd ever think there was such a job."

At that moment Hank and Justin arrived, after a curtesy tap at the front door of the carriage-house. The trio of good looking young guys sauntered into the kitchen. Chelsea, Mike and Jack welcomed them, offering drinks and Mike popped the second baking tray into the oven. By the time the boys were settled in the fresh batch of hot scones were served up.

Chelsea noticed something unusual in her friend Justin's face...she claimed loudly,"Look at Justin's eyes, they're practically glowing! It might be the cranberry scones...Or, I bet he's discovered something new about the phantom of the movie set!"

Everyone looked at Justin, whose mouth was so full of buttered scone he couldn't speak.

Chelsea tossed her bouncing red curls and wondered to herself, "Or, has something romantic happened between Hank and Justin at long last? I hope that's it. Or both actually..." She caught Jack's eye and she could tell he was having similar thoughts.

When Justin could finally speak he said, "I don't really have news, just thoughts, things I've been noticing...things coming together in my mind. But they're still on the back burner."

"Well, Just don't let them boil over," Mike chuckled and passed him a glass of ice tea.

Hank settled on a stool at the counter beside Justin, their knees casually touching.

This was noticed by Mike as he bustled around making space for them all and setting out more plates. "Hmmm that's not something I've seen, such casual contact...Certainly Justin dreamed of it, but has been way to shy...I wonder," Mike thought. He curiously eyed Greer who was sitting on Hanks other side, the youth seemed very relaxed, quietly sipping his drink while watching with seeming enjoyment all the friendly chatter around him. If he noticed any new intimacy between Hank and Justin he seemed unconcerned.

The group discussed the movie, the garden and various Nottinghill Lane gossip... Certainly the youngsters all wanted to know more about the body, but they managed for now, to respect that Detective Mike couldn't share much at the moment. So the young people waited to speculate about the mystery copse until after they left the carriage-house and were walking home.

* * *

There was more speculation later that night, when Jack and Mike were settled in bed... speculating about a particular one of the young people.

"That Greer is a bit of a wild card," said Mike.

"I know what you mean, quiet and mysterious...like a cat, a very handsome cat," Jack agreed, he curled in to snuggle with Mike.

"I know he supposedly came here to help and learn garden planning from assisting Hank, that he's getting course credit on Hank's project...But I just wonder," Mike said.

"Wonder what? You think he has some other motive for being here? Like what?"

"Well, first I thought, maybe he had a crush on Hank..."

"I thought so too, but now you don't?"

"Well, Justin and Hank were getting kind of cosy at the counter this evening," Mike said.

"So they were," Jack said happily, "finally, at last, that's so nice for Justin...and Hank too."

"Yes, it is..."

"But what?" Jack asked.

"Well, I'm almost sure Greer could see their... warmth...But he was very blasé, he didn't seem to mind at all."

"So you think he's got some secret plan?" Jack wondered.

"I don't know, he's just new, we don't really know him yet..." Mike murmured.

"Maybe there's a threesome in Hank's future," Jack chuckled.

"I don't know if Justin would like that too much," Mike said. "But I'm just curious, Greer seems nice, but, he is a bit of a mystery."

"Well, I have a mystery right here for you to solve mister," Jack whispered to his sexy lover as he switched the bedside light off.

Chapter 13 - Lights, Camera, Budget

"It's a small budget film, most of the budget is on the lighting designer and the DP - Director of photography... if you haven't got much money, you make the product look as good as it can..." the director James Barker said to the producer. "It can be economically but it can't look cheap. The cinematography has to be beautiful even if we are going digital."

"If you can save money elsewhere, and this DP

makes the product look good, then fine," the small mustachioed man, Max McBride responded in a flowery voice edged with Brooklyn. Despite his hand tailored expensive suits, the man still had rough edges. "The film rushes are looking good. Cal is creating an interesting chemistry with Jessica, the feeling of history. Which makes sense since they have a bit of history."

The directors eyes widened and he looked even closer at the two movie stars faces gazing at each other on the big monitor as they played the scene of a man and a woman, both mature and attractive reminiscing about their past at the very same small hometown hotel bar that their characters had said goodbye in a decade ago... Their past and present colliding, creating a forbidden, intriguing flame between them, as now they were lawyers on opposite sides in the courtroom.

James Barker watched and wondered... "Cal and Jessica have history, romantic history in real life? Must be from a long time ago, like the characters they're playing... Except the lawyer in the movie that Cal is playing doesn't..."

"Doesn't chase after anything in pants like Radcliffe does? Barker, you know actors, they're all pretty flexible. When an attractive young person and the right romantic setting comes along..." McBride spoke with the authority of a master gossip, and himself a gentleman who enjoyed young men...Though McBride himself had never been slightly tempted by a female. "Their past whatever is was, works for our film, that's all, I care about. I admire both of them, their tremendous talent on screen...Off screen they both have their troubles. Hopefully the success of this film will help them, and you, and me — all of us!"

Barker shifted in his seat, he didn't like to be reminded how badly he needed a hit, even a modest one. It either had to be a hit...or it was better it was never completed at all. His attention went back to the new images on the screen, the mirror crashing, the shimmering — shattering of silvered glass, dramatically showering the dark antique hotel bar...the DP had been genius to keep rolling, it looked frightening, and wonderful.

He could use it, the director thought joyfully, one way or another he could make it work.

Decades ago they used to call these "Art films" which meant esoteric scripts and no budget, no studio. Decades before that, there were "B pictures" which meant big studio — but small budget, no big names in the cast, or maybe actors who used to be big names...Those films were training grounds — filler films back when the studios had a monopoly and owned the theaters too. Back before television, in the long ago days when movie theaters were glamorous havens of escape. These days when people could carry movie screens around in their pockets, and mini movie studios too...

What kept you in the upper echelons of a constantly evolving show business were skilled craftsmanship and hopefully a good story to tell. It was always about the new, the now, the next... It was all about illusion. No matter how sincerely writers, stars and producers told you this was a story of truth...it was still a projection and illusion of truth. But still and always a telling a story.

Max McBride was a money man, a business person, a hundred years ago he might have been selling fake medicines from a horse drawn wagon from town to town. All it took was seeing the opportunity and telling a story, or selling one. The reality is he was producing and promoting a product; if a movie's story wasn't as good as it could be, sell the performances, or the uniqueness of the production; the exotic locations, the feuds on the set, the love affairs...like they did with thot old clunker Cleopatra — that multi million dollar disaster. Max was great at selling the public, persuading them to want what he wants them to want; that was his crafty craft. It had made him rich and powerful, and allowed him to play with people and he liked to play and win what ever it took.

"Movies are a risky, risky business," McBride sighed, "kinda gives you a hard-on don't it." He was now thinking of a cold martini waiting in the warm hands of the handsome young man who was waiting for him in the near by lakefront mansion he had rented for duration of filming.

"Risky, exasperating and addicting," Barker sighed, thinking about the next days shooting. And what could go wrong.

"Good thing we both love it," chuckled McBride with his legendary wicked charm.

It always astonished Barker how such a weaselly little man could have such forceful personality, and magnetism... He had to grudgingly admire this balding dynamo either who drew you in, or drove over you. Max was known to have pulled some crazy stunts and dirty tricks to make bad movies into successes at the box-office. Barker wondered how far the producer would go if he thought a film was in trouble?

Beneath the shimmering surface of Hollywood, tough manipulative men and women, like Max McBride were the invisible reality of the business of show business.

"They don't call it Show-Art" as Lily Tomlin famously said.

It seemed as if the director and producer both had put the thought of the dead body discovered on the set out of their minds...after they had talked it through and decided the strategy for now was hush it up as much as possible, which the Mayor and police wanted also for now.

The reality of the miseries day body was mixed up with the movie for now, camouflaged. That wouldn't last for long. But the movie would be wrapped in just another two weeks.

Both men privately thought leaking the mysteries on the set might prove useful later, the grisly world of publicity being what it is...If when the movie was opening it seemed the press or the box office was sluggish, well then...

It was rather cold blooded but, this was business. Sometimes secrets and scandals could be used, these days more than ever.

But even these two hardened professionals had thoughts that crept in the back of their minds in the dark... making them worry, at least a little about why and who had left the bodies discovered on the set of Cal's last picture and now this one. Would there be more?

Was the phantom not just a trickster, but also potentially a murderer?

Both producer and director had skeletons in their closets, they preferred not to join them.

* * *

Cal lay awake in his bed, his right arm under the head of the pretty young man asleep beside him. The cute young actor had been fun. Cal would try to do him some good, he would introduce him to McBride.

Max McBride loved guiding young actors careers, as long as they were grateful enough... After all Cal Radcliffe himself was proof of what McBride's help and friendship could achieve. Success was all about who you knew and how well you knew them.

Well, talent helped too, and most especially—luck.

Cal's luck had trickled out recently. It seemed like his last picture had been cursed with bad luck...Now this one; Songbird, was beginning to be. The girls dead body...another dead body!

If that was going to happen on all his films...he was doomed. He'd go crazy!

No, that wasn't his style! Cal Radcliffe was tough, he'd lasted decades.

He had made his own luck before, and he would again. Cal caressed the pretty boy dreaming next to him, the sexy guy had the youthful ability of sleeping like the dead.

* * *

Not far away, in the quiet bedroom of their carriage house on Nottinghill Lane, Jack Book woke suddenly, startled from his sleep a nightmare.

Jack shuddered at the dream of a faceless phantom all in black attacking him. He tried to put the image of hands at his throat out of his mind. His lover Mike Page rolled over towards him, murmuring, "Cold."

Jack pulled the blanket up and curled warmly around his lover, drawing comfort and calm, from Mike's tall lean body. He was an island of strength in the night ocean of the bed, Jack let his mind be soothed and lulled by the gentle tide of his handsome lover's rhythmic breathing, as he floated off to sleep once more.

But another nightmare was waiting...

Sometime later, in the early hours of the

morning it was Mike's turn to wake up from s dream. This was not a nightmare, just a series of strange surreal images; eyes — lots of large eyes — peering in windows, reflected in a big mirror, like the mirror that fell off the wall of the barroom and shattered. In his dream Mike looked down at the broken bits and pieces to see dozens of eyes looked back up in the shards.

Who did all these watching, staring eyes belong to he wondered?

Who were all these people on the other side of the mirror?

Mike tossed and turned, then settled back next to sleeping Jack. He wasn't afraid. He somehow knew this wasn't an angry mob of eyes. These eyes all belonged to just one person...It was an odd revelation, but still it felt like somewhere in his mind he had fitted something together. This feeling allowed him to sleep again.

In the morning Mike's dream was almost forgotten, until ... as he was shaving in the bathroom. He was standing at the sink when in the mirror he saw behind Jack as he stepped dripping from the shower. His eyes were admiring the trim smooth body of his blonde lover as he toweled dry. He saw his own face in the mirror watching, his own green eyes looking out of the mirror. Images of the dream eyes wafted in his mind.

"Peeping Tom," Jack chuckled. Then he came up behind Mike hugging him around the waist, kissing the back of his neck. For a moment their eyes met in the mirrors reflection of them.

It was then Mike's dream of peering eyes came vividly back to him, and he had an idea. The eyes in his mind floated over the images of different faces, faces he'd seen around lately...an old woman, a 20's something guy, a stiff lawyer type man...a heavy set fellow in work clothes from the crew...a variety of faces, some with glasses, beards or bangs or hats...but the eyes were all the same cold grey. It was an idea, an odd one...he needed to think it over.

"Mike, let's have coffee..." Jack said, "you look like you need it babe."

Chapter 14 - Shot in the Dark

On the way to the movie hotel, Mike asked, "Jack, the woman who takes pictures of the sets and props, and makes notes on the script..."

"You mean Tracy the script supervisor?" Jack responded.

"Yes, she does what exactly?"

"She's kind of a documentarian. She keeps track of any changes in the script, if a line is added or eliminated...so it's current and consistent with what was actually shot."

"And the pictures she takes?"

"Again their for consistency and continuity...her pictures of how the set and props are at she beginning and ending of shooting a scene are a record that can be referred to if they need to reshoot something, the set dressers and prop people know what and where everything was to match it. Chelsea was really interested in what her job was too."

"And the other guy, with the big camera?"

"He's the still photographer, his pictures are the action of, and making of the film, for publicity."

"I'd be interested in seeing some of those pictures, both of their pictures," Mike said.

"I think you only have to ask," Jack smiled.

"Thanks, I will see them in while, I'm watching over Cal's first scene this morning in the barroom."

Mike strolled beside Jack in the morning light. They were shooting interiors so the day was starting later 8am instead of the 5 or 6am call daylight exteriors usually were.

It was quiet in their lane and on the town streets, until they came closer to the hotel and the assembly of cars and trucks in its parking lot, there activity was already beginning. They greeted a small group of crew getting breakfast at the catering truck.

Mike took his coffee off to check in with Cal. Jack spotted Jessica and carried his tea over to chat with her.

Mike liked to scope out the sets and hotel looking for any signs of potential trouble, and Cal liked to have the detectives reassuring presence around. Mike had become a sometime sounding board for Cal. Which Mike had come to enjoy to some degree, he was canny enough to see the insecure lonely person wrapped in the glib lascivious movie star.

Later in the day Jack had a small scene with

Jessica, who was so unnerved by the mishaps on the film, she begged him to run lines and rehearse with her beforehand. Which he was happy to do.

Jack felt her fragility, he had seen her trembling hands on the set. Was there more it then her nerves he wondered...her assistant Whitney was so watchful, hovering like a nurse or a jailer.

Jack laughed when Jessica commented on the vitality of two young production assistants playing frisbee on the lawn..."I look at young people sometimes and I feel like a vampire," she said wistfully, "I want to suck the energy and flexibility right out of them."

Her lovely face smiled with humor, but in her eyes was something more serious, a hunger, a longing.

"But you're not old," Jack rushed to say.

"I feel old..." the still beautiful actress said, "this business...its a vampire, sucking the life out of you..." Suddenly the gloom of her mood lifted, "but it gives life too. I love it... And this film of ours Jack is the beginning of my reinvention. I'm going to... going to..." her voice faltered. "I might get fat! Very fat..." Jack was startled to hear Jessica say with glee.

She glanced at his stunned face, "Oh, silly, I just mean I might stray a tiny bit from my diet and have some ice cream or egg rolls or lots of French fries...Its been years." The slender actress chuckled, but then her eyes lighted with dreams, "Really Jack I do have plans, if all goes well..."

Jack was on the edge of his seat waiting to hear what she was planning to do. She told him of her hopes for future roles and a streaming series...A play in London perhaps. "One of my early films was shot in England at Pinewood Studios."

"Red Sky At Night - I love that film," Jack said.

"Did you know James Barker our esteemed director worked on that film. He was only a second Assistant then... He didn't used to bark back then. Now he lives up to his name. But... then...he was much younger, determined that he would make great art, make beautiful meaningful films that would change the world..." Jessica's low wistful voice was mesmerizing as spoke her of memories.

Was this part of her preparation process Jack wondered, not that he cared. He was a very willing audience. He could listen to her deep succulent voice all day... she had a wonderful voice, a distinctive voice...like certain British actresses had, like old movie stars used to have...not the indistinguishable untrained voices of many young American actresses these days.

Together they walked to the production trailers to get into wardrobe and make up.

"Oh here we are, well thanks for letting me bend your ear Jack. See you on the set," she smiled and he opened the metal door for her.

* * *

The first scene of the day, had Cal again in the bar. His lawyer character meeting with the hostess to explain details of his clients actions on the night the waitress was strangled. The hostess was going to be sitting answering his questions about the accused young man who worked in the bar...and that night. There was a bartender behind them silently wiping glasses.

The room's windows were blacked out, with lighting artificially made to stream in through blinds to look as if it were late afternoon, even though outside it was just ten in the morning. The room had a dusky atmosphere.

The crew and cameras were ready, and a voice called out, "Quiet on the set! Rolling! Take one! Action!"

Cal lit cigarettes for both of them, then leaned in quietly asking, "Is this the same bar our lady prosecutor sings at sometimes?" he asked.

"Yes," answered the hostess, "But she wasn't singing here that night, at least I don't think she was..."

"But your not sure?" he asked.

"Why, does it matter?" The tall svelte brunette responded.

"Maybe, I'm not sure what matters yet. I just want to know the facts," the actor's low voice rasped.

Suddenly the lights went out! The room was night black!

In the dark there was a thunderous bang and bright sparking flash ...a gun shot. Amidst the screams and yells someone crashed to floor.

* * *

Jack heard a commotion inside the hotel. He saw some of the crew rushing out of the doors. Everyone was running and stumbling and on their cell phones. Moments later an ambulance came roaring up lights and siren flashing. The medics rushed into the building.

Jack asked some of the stunned crew what had happened? One of the female PAs gasped, there'd been a gun shot.

"Someone tried to shoot Cal Radcliffe I think," she said looking pale.

Jack was watching the hotel's main entrance, as police cars pulled up with more flashing lights. A crowd was gathering on the street.

Moments later the gurney was wheeled out with someone loaded on it.

But it wasn't the movie star, it was his lover Mike!

* * *

At the hospital it had taken a while to sort out what had exactly happened and what Mike's condition was.

Fortunately Mike hadn't sustained any serious injuries. He had only damaged himself in the fall as he had once again hurled himself at Cal Radcliffe to thrust him out of harms way. But in the darkness he had managed to cut his shoulder on a bottle that broke in the commotion. It wasn't a bullet after all, much to Jack's relief. Mike had however also knocked his head on the brass football of the bar and passed out for a few minutes. So the doctor was inviting he stay in the hospital over night for observation as a precaution, in case he had a concussion. Mike had protested vigorously. However, the films producer insisted for insurance purposes that he should. Jack had insisted as well.

Once Mike's struggling to get up and out was over, he had surrendered to the mandated rest in bed. His body counter acted the adrenaline burst generated in his reaction to the shot in the dark and getting the star out of harms way, he fell quickly and deeply asleep right before Jack's eyes.

Jack sat by Mike's bedside, watching his slumber. He stared at his lover's taped forehead and bandaged shoulder, one of the broad shoulders he so admired, and felt a spiral of fear and huge relief, so happy Mike would be all right, so upset that he had been hurt and wounded. As a coping distraction he pulled out his sketchbook and began to draw his brave sleeping lover.

As his pencil moved across the paper drawing his lover, random thoughts skittered across Jack's still flustered mind: I am short, Mike is tall. I am blond, Mike's hair dark. He is brave and I am fearful a lot of the time...but now he loves me and I'm less afraid. Except now I'm afraid for him...but he's Okay! Thank god he's Okay... Jack reassured himself as his shock was wearing off.

Jack thought of how they were so different, opposite in many ways, but remarkably they fit together, like a pair of gloves opposites, a team, perfect together. Jack smiled at himself and flipped to a fresh page of his sketchbook...Mike Page...his detective...his answer to the confounding mystery of love.

Well, maybe each could do well on their own,

better then one shoe or a lone glove...but as a pair they were...miraculous. Jack did feel finding each other in the confusion of the world was a kind of miracle. He was grateful, profoundly grateful. And he thought together they had created magic in the world; making art, restoring gardens, solving riddles and of course Mike's funny magic tricks. He called them illusions but they were magic to Jack.

As he was shading Mike's eyelids, they fluttered open revealing two dark green question marks. "Hey handsome," rasped Mike's voice softly, " I was dreaming about you..."

"And I was daydreaming about you, Mr. Hero, " Jack responded.

"Any word yet on the gun and the shooter?" Mike asked slightly groggy.

Jack gave him a glass of ginger ale, "Well, it turns out the phantom struck again. They think it was just a prop gun that shot a blank. The prop master found his gun box lock jimmied, and a revolver missing along with some black ammunition."

"Not so much a hero then, though blanks can still be dangerous," Mike said.

"Blanks certainly can be," Jack agreed thinking of movie set accidents with blanks he'd heard about. He'd always been nervous when he'd had to use prop guns on project he'd acted in. "But I'm grateful that's what it was and not live bullets."

Jack started to tear up just at the thought of what might have been.

"Babe, come on don't cry, I'm fine," Mike reassured caressing Jack's hand, then squeezing it.

"I know, its just..."

"Hey, come on...as long as I'm in bed for the afternoon, I have an idea..."

"Mike, you need to rest," Jack chuckled as naughty thoughts danced in his head.

"What I was thinking was, you could tell me one of your wonderful stories...for now anyway," Mike smiled a slow sexy heroic smile, "When I get home however..."

Chapter 15 - Movie Mosaic

A few days later Mike was just a little sore from his wound. He bounced back to work with resiliency. However, the brief forced rest and distance from the production had given him time to think over the puzzle of the movies real life mysteries.

He felt like he was looking down at a table top of mosaic pieces as he gazed at the borrowed photos of the production, and at the neat index cards of notes he had spread out before him. As mosaic tiles that would fit together in a pattern, a design of facts that would illuminate who was behind all the crimes and mischief that had plagued the movie production.

Or should he be thinking of it as a recipe? Ingredients for mystery?

Jack came up behind him and slipped his arms around his lover, nibbling his neck, then almost as if reading his mind he asked, "Are you sorting out your recipe cards?"

Mike caressed the hands encircling his waist thoughtfully, "Not for cooking, these are notes about this crime spree on the film. I'm trying to see the pattern, trying to put a picture together. But it is like a recipe or a mosaic," he explained.

"Or like...one of your magic tricks?" Jack suggested, "Misdirection?Getting the audience to look the other way." His word sparked a memory in Mike of the odd dream he'd had of eyes, the many eyes reflected in the mirrors broken shards, that he somehow thought were all one...

His hands shuffled through the photographs, his own sharpe eyes searching here and there, reflections and eyes... many but all one.

"The many that are one..." he murmured.

"Is that a quote?" Jack asked very curious what was brewing in his lover's astute brain.

"No, but it might just be the password to this mystery," he answered,

"Jack you know how you told me the importance in art of the observing the shapes and spaces between objects?"

Jack nodded.

"Well, Look here," Mike's finger pointed out a detail in one of the set photos, and here, and over here..."

Jack began to see. And what he saw confirmed the idea he's had after his nightmare with the eyes...the vague ideas he's had about how the phantom worked now seemed confirmed by Mike's evidence.

* * *

Great ideas often occur to more then one person at the same time, and so it happened that

Mike and Jack were not the only ones was putting some similar pieces together...

* * *

However, it also happens, some not so great ideas are put into motion sometimes too...

Chelsea's plan to get an interview with the movie star Cal Radcliffe, was maybe, not the best idea...

Nonetheless...one afternoon she and Hank found themselves in the hotel parking lot, outside the dressing room trailer the target of her interview.

Chelsea's watchful eyes did catch a glimpse of the quaint old lady she'd noticed on her first day off filming... but she was too excited and nervous about her plan to get her interview with Cal Radcliffe to wonder what she was doing outside his trailer...Hank accompanied her. And his handsome presence worked as she had hoped it would. The movie stars eyes lighted up with delight as they skimmed past the perky red haired girl proceeding to rapidly savor every detail of Hanks athletic blonde deliciousness.

"Mr. Radcliffe I'm Chelsea, I'm a freelance journalist writing about your film and this Hank my Photographer, and I was hoping we might have just a few minutes of your time..."

Again the movie stars eyes devouringly zeroed in on the very stunning young man holding a camera beside the girl. He quickly calculated the ratio of the boredom of answering interview questions, versus the excitement offered by the hot guy — He took in the tall, lean, blonde youth who looked exactly like one of his fantasies come to life, and he had to stop himself from drooling, "Well, young lady I believe I might snatch a bit of time for an enterprising young reporter and her photographer..."

In moments they were welcomed in to the trailer, with Hank playing his part as her photographer perfectly. At Radcliffes urging to feel free to take as many pictures as he wanted. Using the camera landscaping works with snapped the actors image. The star elatedly posed affecting different attitudes and characters, all the while edging closer and closer to Hank...

Chelsea peppered him with a scatter-shot of questions all the while, asking about his early days in the theater and his stories about various of his major successes.

Hank for his part was enjoying what was to him a bit a harmless game, and helping his friend Chelsea. He hadn't thought her plan would actually work, but the interest he was getting from Cal proved it had. Hank was not star struck, but still found it very interesting to meet in parson the actor he'd seen in so many movies. Though he wasn't a particularly handsome man, he did exude a certain magnetism.

At a certain point when the Cal insisted Hank sit next to him and show him in the cameras viewer the pictures he'd taken so far, he was snuggled right up against Hank. There faces very close looking at the small pictures.

"You're very good," Cal complimented. "I really like that one! And, that one, very nice too," his voice was syrupy and playful. He then suggested, "I like to take photos too, why don't you let me take some of you...Turn-about is fair. You've inspired me."

Radcliffe proceeded to take the camera and focus it on Hanks chiseled face, for a very close, close up. "Tell me about yourself young man..." he purred clicking away, as Hank obligingly leaned back on the couch and smiled. He thought this movie stars moves were pretty funny.

"Your eyes are so blue, Hank that's your name isn't it? Sky blue, I could just fly away in them." The movie star was now practically on top of Hank as he snapped picture after picture.

Though Chelsea was still managing to get an occasional answer from Cal she was thought things were getting out of control...her plan was working too well. But she found herself hypnotized watching the movie star maneuvering to entice her handsome friend. It was a bit comical, Hanks very tall leanly muscular body being compelled to lean farther and farther back as the not so tall, slightly pudgy slight balding actor tried to entangle him like a python...

Suddenly it all climaxed just as Radcliffe was attempting to unbutton Hanks shirt with one hand while holding the camera with the other while strategically rubbing his groin up against Hanks crotch...

There was a pounding knock at the door, which was then opened to reveal Greer peering in, with Duane Cal's assistant struggling to keep him from entering.

At which point Hank could no longer contain himself and burst into laughter. Causing Chelsea to snap out of her trance. Radcliffe slid back off Hank, rapidly slid down his legs to the floor as

Hank grabbed the camera from his hand.

"Hank, Chelsea! Your both needed for another story! Urgently!" Greer cried out, beckoning them out of the seduction scene, as he pushed The pesky assistant away. His strong right arm easily holding him at bay. Which as Duane took in just how cute Greer was he struggled less and less.

Like a super hero metamorphosing Greer hustled his friends out the stars trailer den of iniquity and lust into his waiting car and drove them away... leaving in their wake the star and his assistant both aroused, disappointed and somewhat baffled.

"But wow that Hank was hot!" Cal exclaimed to Duane.

"So was the other one," sighed the assistant.

Neither was sorry to have had at least some physical encounter with the beautiful young men, how ever brief.

"I just keep my eyes open," Greer explained

as the three were safely sipping sodas at the Dockside, a near by cafe. "Hank told me your plan Chelsea, and I just wanted to watch out for you. Ever since Hank started telling me about his interesting friends on Nottinghill Lane, I wanted to come meet you all. I've grown to feel like your a little family, one I'd like to be part of..." his gentle low voice sounded shy.

"Well, I can't thank you enough," Chelsea told him. Her expression sincere and relieved, "Things wen't beyond what was thinking..."

"Thanks from me too," Hank said. "I didn't want to have to do anything drastic to get that guy off me, Boy what a horny old dog. I hope almost scarifying my manly virtue got you the story you wanted Chelsea."

"Well, I'm not sure what I'll write, but it won't be an expose. I don't like that kind of writing. But he did tell me a few things about his early life while he was hovering over you. And I can't wait to see your pictures..." the red haired girl grinned,"and the ones he took of you Hank!"

They all rehashed the entire crazy movie star adventure over, each telling their version from their view point. In the end Chelsea swore the two boys to secrecy about it, as it was not her finest moment either as a reporter or friend, although it increased her appreciation of Hank and Greer by a thousand percent.

Chelsea began to look at Greer in a new way, curious to know more about what he was like besides being a darkly handsome guy. She began to think of him apart from being Hanks side kick.

From some of the looks he gave her over the rest of the afternoon she began to think maybe he was interested in getting to know her better. Maybe much better, which she wouldn't mind at all.

Chapter 16 - Multiple Personalities

He's a nerdy, a bit like a wilted lettuce leaf or tulip, Chelsea thought. There was a particularly usual, young guy she had noticed. Who very unusual for an actor or extra... seemed like he was not trying very hard to not be noticed!

In a room full of actor types was odd, and she thought interesting and with making note of in her notes, even sneaking a few covert photos.

In a way she thought he seemed empty, seemed as though he was waiting for some passing the spirit to possess in him and give him some personality. She was trying not to stare but she fascinated watching someone be practically invisible to everyone but her. She had also noticed he seemed to disappear from the holding tent a lot. But then it was a frenetic busy place. He also seemed to not be working everyday, there were several people who seemed to pop in and out. But when she asked Ben one of the downstate veterans of the film business, he said it wasn't particularly unusual. People came and went depending on whether casting called them and their availability, it was all very random.

Chelsea made note of that in her journal for her film essay. She also made some notes of other people that she was thinking of who popped in and out; the Miss Marple-like old woman from the first day, the young blonde punky guy and the silver haired lawyer type. What was it about them that was in the back of her mind that these disparate characters had in common...maybe nothing, but still she was sure there was something odd about all of them. Were they all part of a plot, like in books she had read?

Well, this is real life, she told herself. Then she laughed and Justin sitting next to her asked what was funny.

"I was just thinking this is real life, when right now, us working on this movie seems like anything but real life," she answered. I have to remember to sneak some more pictures of all these characters, she thought.

"It is a pretty strange kind of reality, working to make a movie seem real. I never thought what an army of people it takes to do it," Justin said gazing around the tent at all the make up, hair dressers and wardrobe people engaged in busily working or lounging, rushing or waiting as needs demanded.

Along with many others moving in and out of the vast tent were; catering staff refreshing Craft Service the tables of snacks, production assistants with their breakdowns of the todays and tomorrows scenes — seeing who would be needed, and when, in order to be ready for various calls to various sets...as well as all the extras, there were fewer today only twenty at the moment, but there could be more for a later call time.

* * *

Upstairs on the third floor of the hotel, far away from the bustle of the production Jessica Zane was giving an interview. She had just about had it with this intrusive reporter and his questions. Also the fact that skinny narrow faced fellow resembled a weasel in glasses. He was making her feel like she was being visited by a character from Wind In The Willows.

The reporter had started out nice enough, asking about her recent movies and her role in this film. But then her patience was worn thin as his questions become more scatter shot...about her work with Cal in the past...and rumors about his sexuality, and had there been trouble on the set of this film? She bunted he answers...

Jessica explained she really didn't know Cal

Radcliffe all that well. Yes, they had worked together once, years ago... (She had almost slipped and said tears ago, it hadn't been the happiest of experiences her brief tryst with Cal. But she certainly was keeping mum about that piece of ancient history)

"I respect Mr. Radcliffe as an actor and a professional," Jessica said putting on her most politic voice, "But beyond that, we're friendly on the set, but were not really friends..."

Is my hand getting a tremble? Is it noticeable? She wondered.

"And the director James Barker, he's know to be a bit of an obsessive demon...and you sometimes seem to be...fragile. Were't you replaced on the film - Smoke at Dawn because of an issue." The slender fellow asked eyeing his phone recording their conversation on the table next to him.

The actress responded cooly, "Sometimes you don't realize a film isn't the right fit for you until too late..."

At that moment the ever vigilant Whitney who

had been observing attentively by the door, intervened.

"I am sorry Mr. Robinson that's all the time for questions Miss Zane has time for. If you've finished your coffee, I'll escort you out." She smiled icily. "If you'd like to take some of the fruit or cookies from the tray with you I have a doggie bag at hand for you." She produced the bag and filled it up with pastries neither she or Jessica would want, and the scrawny guy could probably use. Also she wanted to both seem generous and make him feel a bit scruffy.

The man scrambled to pack up his shoulder bag with his notebook and phone, then rose and sheepishly accepted the offered bag. He felt he was being brushed off, but he was suddenly feeling unwell, a bit nauseous and unsteady. Reporter Robinson hastily said good-bye and thanked Jessica for her time, then hurriedly left with Whitney escorting him as far as the end of the hall. She watched him begin to descend the hotel grand old staircase, before she turned to go back to the suite.

Whitney returned certain Jessica would need her to fix her a soothing drink, as she reentered the room she said, "That guy seemed a bit of a weasel." Jessica laughed out loud that the semblance she thought was apparent to Whitney.

She was about to agree with her... when they heard a crash! Followed by the sounds of a great commotion coming from far down the corridor.

"You stay where you are Jessie! I'll go see what's going on out there. Lock the door after me, just in case," Whitney said as she briskly left the room. "After the other day, we can't take any chances."

Jessica was trying to hold off on having her whiskey till later, so she eyed the tray of refreshments that a maid had set up before the interview to see if there was anything else she could have for now. The coffee pot was thermal so it would still be warm...What if she had a coffee and just spiked it a tiny bit? She found the hip flask in her purse and added a splash. She was about to take a sip when Whitney knocked for her to unlock the door.

"What on earth was that?" Jessica asked as she reseated herself on the couch and lifted the cup from the coffee table.

"Don't drink that!" yelled Whitney, as she strode over grabbing the cup and saucer and replacing it on the tray.

"Why? Whatever is it? What's wrong with the coffee?"

"The reporter who was just here, he's collapsed on the stairs and fallen down them. Mike the detective happened to be right there, he thinks the guy might possibly have poisoned!"

"Is he dead?" Jess asked aghast.

"No, he's just very ill, and battered from the fall. But I told Detective Mike that he had just drunk coffee here," Whitney told her.

The two women exchanged shocked, anxious glances as they processed this latest catastrophe. They stared at the tray on the coffee-table as though it was full of snakes.

After a while there was a knock at the door, Whitney let the Detective in with another deputy. He surveyed the tray still sitting just as they'd left it. Jessie had moved herself away from it to on the window seat, but had been staring at wondering if poison was in everything on the tray; the coffee, tea, milk and the cookies? She had poured a cup of tea which she hadn't drunk. The actress had drunk her bottled water instead.

"Do you think it was me someone wanted to poison Detective?" Jessica asked.

"That would be my first thought," he answered.

"You certainly don't suspect Jessica or me of poisoning a reporter..." Whitney asked a bit incredulous, "even if he was rather annoying."

Mike responded, "Well, though we do have to keep an open mind, I would think if that were the case, you would have left a long trail of dead reporters by now in your business. Unless of course, there was something in particular about this... Mr. Robinson. Had you met him before?"

"Never, he was from a Traverse City local newspaper, not a national. It's not likely Jessica would have encountered him on a press junket in the past," Whitney interjected.

"I assume this was his cup?" The detective asked.

Jessica nodded yes, Mike turned to the other officer,"Johnson, can you bag everything on this tray and take it to the lab. Was there anything you noticed about him?"

"The lab sir?" The officer looked puzzled.

"Well, call Dr. Mitch and ask if he could test to figure out what it was and what it was in."

"Right Mike."

The detective looked back at Jessica and Whitney.

"You asked if there was anything I noticed, well he did look a bit ... a bit like a weasel. Otherwise he seemed to get a bit pushy and invasive in his questions toward the end of our interview." Jessica answered, "But he was just rather ordinary." Then she added thoughtfully, "Wait, now that I think about it, there was something odd..."

"What was odd about him?" Mike asked.

"No, it wasn't Mr. Robinson... There was something odd about the maid that brought the coffee tray. But I'm not sure I can put my finger on it. She was in and out very quickly," she said.

Whitney chimed in agreeing, "I know, it didn't occur to me till now. But she didn't seem like the regular hotel staff. Her uniform, her manner, it was as if she were acting a part, like in an old movie. It didn't hit me until this minute. And I did think she had rather large feet. I remember thinking her shoes looked like the big cloddy shoes Nuns at my Catholic school wore. But then she would wear serviceable shoes wouldn't she?"

Mike sat with the two women and took some more notes, trying also to reassure them. While he was there the deputy took a call and passed along a status update, the reporter was doing all right at the hospital. He wasn't critical.

"It could have just been food poisoning Mike, something he ate earlier," the officer conjectured.

"That possible Johnson," Mike said, "but with what's been going on this film recently..." Unconsciously he rubbed his recently wounded shoulder, "I'll feel better when all these coffee tray samples have been checked out."

"Detective, do you mind if I excuse myself for a minute. I'd like to wash my hands and change," Jessica asked.

"Not at all, go right ahead Miss Zane," Mike answered politely.

"Thank you, and call me Jessica, please."

"I'll come with you Jess," Whitney offered, and they passed into the bedroom of the suite.

"Almost packed up Johnson?" Mike asked, looked at the carefully assembled plastic-bagged items from the tray, now all carefully packed in a box. "What about the tray? It won't fit in the box Mike. But I can get a garbage bag to put the tray in, will that be okay?"

Before Mike had time to answer... loud, piercing screams erupted from the other room, where both the movie star and her assistant were shrieking with terror!

Chapter 17 - Another Body

Mike and Johnson sprinted into the bedroom, shocked to see a dead body sprawled on the carpet. A young woman with a red scarf around her neck. Another dead girl!

A very frightened Jessica exclaimed, "She just...I just opened my closet, and it just fell out!"

"Holy smokes! Another corpse!" exclaimed Johnson.

Beside him Mike was thinking a stronger curse word, but settled for murmuring, "Damn it." Then the detective said,"Call it in Johnson, and see who's still downstairs from the reporter's accident. There's probably some officers who can cover the door and lock up this scene for us.

* * *

A short while later, Mike sat with the star and her assistant after having escorted the ladies safely away the crime scene downstairs to a library off the main lobby of the hotel.

As Jessica and Whitney both were sipping restorative glasses of whisky. The two women explained, prior to the reporter's interview, they had both been away from the suite all morning, downstairs in the bar rehearsing Jessica's song for the scene she was going to be shooting in a few days. Afterwards there was a final wardrobe fitting for the costume. So they hadn't been back upstairs till shortly before the reporter was due to arrive.

"And you were with Miss Zane the entire time Miss?" Mike asked Whitney.

"Well, yes. I mean I was in and out on a few

different errands, but never for very long," she explained.

"That's right Detective, she was never gone for more than a few minutes at a time," Jessica agreed, "certainly not long enough to..." her voice trailed off.

"I'm not suggesting anything, just trying to get the timings. How long the suite was empty?" he enquired as he made notes.

"That's hard to say exactly, some hours...I might have popped in and out to retrieve something Jess needed..." the assistant answered.

"That poor girl, lured up there and strangled," Jessica said shivering.

"That might not be the case," Deputy Johnson said before stopping himself and looking guiltily at Mike, who shot him a warning look.

"You mean she was already dead," Jessica gasped horrified, "but how...why...? It doesn't make any sense. Why me? Why my suite?"

"And who was she?" Whitney asked.

"These are all questions to be answered," Mike said, "for now, your suite is a crime scene. You will have to be in another room at least for the foreseeable future."

"Another room? I'd prefer we find another hotel altogether...I would prefer not to be murdered!"she said.

Mike decided he would share just a bit about the bodies, he suspected this corpse also was another stolen from awaiting burial...not murdered. Just another scare tactic. Once the movie star heard these new facts, she took a moment, she then gathered her strength, "No, no! I won't be bullied by some crazy buffoon! We'll stay here. The filming will go on! It must go on, jobs, money, careers demand it!" she said dramatically, and felt it, tossing her hair defiantly, eyes glowing, radiant, "I just need another whisky..."

"You can take my room, and I have night things and clothes," Whitney said, "may we go now detective Mike? I'm sure Jessica needs to rest."

"Of course," Mike said, "and there will be a policeman on guard in the hall and patrolling the grounds night and day."

The pair of women looked relieved to hear that. Mike watched them walk away hoping they would be able to sleep. He admired the assistants efficient and caring manner.

* * *

Much, much with Mike and Jack wine glasses in hand, visited the hidden garden behind the carriage house in Nottinghill Lane and breathed in the cool evening air as they walked in the fading sunset. They strolled the beautiful secret garden that had been rediscovered and recently been given new life. The lovers found it a wonderful retreat from the world both for romance and rumination. As they strolled the paths and observed the new spring stirrings and greening, they discussed the latest twisting link in the chain of strange events on the movie location.

"This latest body, was she another stolen corpse accessorized to look like a victim from the script?" Jack asked.

"She was — is. The corpse just popped out of Jessica Zane's closet. It almost fell right on top of her and her assistant," Mike answered.

Jack pictured the hotel, and the suite. He was familiar with its general layout,"How on earth did someone manage to get a heavy body in and up to the third floor at all, let alone without anyone seeing it?"

"That is the question, one of them anyway," Mike said with a sigh,"the only people who had been around the room near the time were the reporter who ended up in the hospital and a shifty missing maid that the hotel knows nothing about, which makes her very suspect."

"Could a woman do this? A body is very heavy. Well, of course women can do anything really... That is if it was a woman. But I wonder, the big shoes you told me about, and how oddly theatrical the maid seemed, make me think it is a man disguised who did this."

"I agree, that's likely. I have a few thoughts about how it might have been done," Mike said. As they walked around the central fountain, not yet turned on, they the sat on its ledge, their eyes sweeping over the garden and its high ivy covered walls.

After a moment or two of thoughtful silence, (or as silent as the great out doors can be with evening breeze whispering in the branches, crickets chirping here and there and a few squirrels and birds still about) Jack who had been imagining how he might manage maneuvering a dead body up three stories, leaned into his lovers ear and whispered, "If I were the phantom, I know what I would do..."

Despite the fact the Jack's warm breath in his ear was prompting him to want to investigate other things with Jack, in a low sexy growl he asked, "So what have to come up with darling? You tell me your theory and I'll tell you mine.

Then, maybe you'll get a reward."

"The summer house is right over there, with a cushy couch, you could reward me first..." Jack teased, kissing Mike's neck.

"Tell me first, you have to earn your reward."

"So masterful," Jack chuckled.

Mike pinched his lover's cute bottom, "You know it."

"All right, well......I'm thinking...several things, the most complicated is somehow managing to use the camera crane in the parking lot to hoist the body to a window of the suite conveniently left open..."

"Well, I applaud your imagination, go on... theory two?" Mike asked.

"A bell hop disguise and a luggage trolly and a trunk...... "

"How does he get it up those three grand flights of historic stairs?" Mike asked.

"Well, may you ask. I happen to know there is old hidden a service elevator accessible from the basement. It's going to be renovated to be a handicap lift for when the hotel reopens after renovation, after the film is finished. The money from the film is paying for most of it. Anyway... the bell hop could use it. Or if he or she was dressed as film crew there are these long black canvas bags used for lighting set ups that would be perfect. But last and not least is my favorite — following the line of thought of someone disguised as a maid, they could use a big industrial laundry cart. The body if too stiff to fold, could be covered with laundry and maybe an ironing board."

"All of your theories are interesting..." Mike said chuckling softly, but he wasn't dismissive. Then he said thoughtfully,"Would there be an ironing board in a laundry cart?"

"Maybe not usually, but I think it makes sense by association, laundry - I mean there would be sheets and towels piled up. If any one asked, which I doubt, the maid could just say — some fuss budget wants their sheets ironed."

"Really, people actually iron their sheets?"

"I kid you not, the Duchess of Windsor had her sheets ironed twice a day." Jack informed Mike with a knowledgeable grin. "She had them ironed when the bed was made in the morning, and again in the afternoon, after her nap."

"How strange are the rich are...ironing things over and over as if it would iron out their problems..." Mike sighed, "I didn't know about the service elevator. How could I not know that?"

"Well, it's old and not used much, it's hidden in the back of the staff supply closets on each floor. The one I peeked into had a lot of stuff piled in front of the door. The door is just an old wooden door, but when you open it, there is an old folding metal gate." Jack explained.

"How did you find it anyway?" Mike wondered.

"Well, as you've seen by now there's a lot of wait time between setups and camera moves. I got bored waiting one day and was just exploring...Really, I was looking for a cozy place for us to make out sometime..."Jack smiled, "Also, while waiting I was chatting with the bartender, who actually is the hotel bartender, and he told me about an old dumbwaiter behind the kitchen. Not only that, but there's supposedly some tunnels and maybe secret passages from back in prohibition days to sneak booze in and out."

"Curiouser and curiouser, certainly good for phantom sneaking about," Mike murmured running his fingers through Jack's thick blonde hair. "Much more to check out. But a dumbwaiter? The body would have to standing upright. That doesn't seem practical."

"Not for that, but for other phantom tricks maybe. Anyway, I like the maid with the laundry cart and the service elevator."

"Plausible, it's all tricky, risky, but possible. But that still leaves us with who?" Mike said.

"Well, you know how you've told me to be suspicious of who finds the body, so I thought maybe either Jessica or Whitney could have done it."

"Or both of them, the two of them could have

set it up more easily. But why? Why have a body in your own room, to look innocent when they discover it?"

"But what is their motive? I think Jessica really needs this role and the movie to succeed," Jack said, "now, I do like the idea of Whitney being able to disguise herself as the maid in a way that even Jessica doesn't recognize her. Agatha Christie always held that maids were more or less invisible, in hotels anyway."

"I don't think that's true these days, and not in the United States..." Mike said, "Besides, my read on Whitney is she's devoted to Jessica Zane."

"Is that what the kids are calling it these days... devotion?"chuckled suggestively Jack.

Mike's brows rose in surprise, "What? You mean the two of them?"

Jack nodded, "I think they've become more than friends. They've been glowing and touching a lot lately. And I'm glad, especially now, they can comfort and support each other."

"Speaking of comforting my darling, I think I

hear the cozy couch in the summerhouse calling us," Mike pulled his handsome young lover to his feet and guided him to their garden love-nest, "don't forget your wineglass."

"But I'm out of wine," Jack said.

"Some clever person stashed a bottle there earlier, just in case."

"My detective, always one step ahead," Jack grinned. And soon they were happily ensconced in candlelight, sipping more cabernet and kissing, and sipping, sipping and kissing.

And then, they put their glasses down, and then... Jack received his very big reward from Mike for all his interesting theories.

Night came, bringing stars and glowing moonlight and the sing song of crickets, as well as a scattering of glittering fireflies.

Chapter 18 - Deadly Friendship

The next morning, out of blue the Jack said, "I think friendship can be deadly."

Mike looked at his lover in the kitchen sunlight with a startled glance as he set down a rack of toast, responding "That was a random morning thought."

Buttering a slice of the hearty wheat bread toasted crispness, he explained, "I had this weird dream last night about being on the movie set, and I was in a war zone between the trailers, the makeup trailer and the prop trailer and the wardrobe trailer were all battling each other."

Mike sipped his coffee and mused, "And it's not like that in reality?"

"We're all a team with a common goal," Jack said idealistically. "Of course, there are factions and petty rivalries like anywhere else...and sometimes friends are not what they seem."

Mike eyed him with his green lie detector eyes, "Like any where else? Is a movie set like anywhere else?"

"Well, not really, everything on a movie is more heightened by the pressures of production, and the tensions of art versus business," Jack admitted.

"Who won the dream battle?"

"Well, the make up people were shooting lipstick missiles at the wardrobe costume zombies. I was reporting on it into my phone like a correspondent for The Hollywood war reporter, then Cal Radcliffe floated down on a cloud with the booming voice of god, declaring he was the king and all must bow to him."

Mike grinned as he poured Jack another cup of

coffee, "So this wasn't so much a dream as your subconscious replaying realty on the set..."

Jack yawned, then his eyes went dreamy as he tried to recall an elusive detail, "There was a hooded terrorist, appearing behind all the fighters urging them on."

Mike looked interested,"Man or woman?"

Jack thought for a moment, "Well, it kept morphing into different shapes with different faces male, female, young and old — shape shifting, but the dark hood was always masking it. Sometimes the hood was in a suit, others a dress, others...a uniform..."

"A uniform..." Mike echoed...

Jack's eyes refocused as he reached for another slice of toast, "But this phantom was using both departments, wardrobe and make up... And this is very strange, you know how funny you think it is that the toilet trailer instead of Men and Women is labeled Lucy and Desi? Well, the phantom was going in and out of both Desi and Lucy." Jack grimaced, "It seemed wrong...

somehow it wasn't trans-gender… more like devious."

"Well, it sounds…at least indecisive" Mike laughed, "but it's oddly interesting," he said thoughtfully, then asked, "How about a little yogurt and fruit?"

Just then the doorbell rang, starling them both. Mike opened the front door to find the excitable duo of young Chelsea and Justin.

Justin: I admit I like popping in on Jack and Mike unexpectedly, kind of like a sneak inspection, to see if their relationship is a dreamy as it seems…I love that it is.

It gives me hope and something to believe in.

Chelsea: This time we had something urgent to share with them.

The two young people burst into the kitchen like a pair of mini tornados, whirling and twirling their arms, dangling iPhones and other assorted paraphernalia. Both of them talking at once, "We think we know!"

"There's people, and then there's not! Do you see?" Chelsea exclaimed breathlessly.

"We think we might know who is the phantom, who it is, or who they might be, maybe more than one," Justin eagerly and confusingly explained.

"Whoa, whoa, slow down you two. Settle down, have some coffee, take some deep breaths, then start over and go slow," Mike directed, easing them to the seats at the counter. Jack knew how they liked their coffee and had it standing by. A few minutes and a few sips later, they began again.

"You go first Chelsea, it's really your theory," Justin offer politely, "I'll bring up the pictures." He took his laptop from his should bag and opened it on the counter.

Jack and Mike leaned in curious to see and hear.

"Well, I have been documenting the movie

behind the scenes as you know, and I have to be pretty covert sometimes, because the film doesn't want any images or information to get out that isn't approved." She tossed her red ringlets in a rebellious manner, self assured that as a writer reporting rules aren't the same for her."So I have candid shots of a lot of the people around the film.

A lot of the background extras, who are bored and do all sorts of kookie things in the holding tent. There were certain people that I noticed because they didn't seem to want to be noticed. Also, who seemed quietly there, and then not there. One little grey haired old lady, with a hat with a red silk flower. She was reading curled in a corner for a long time, with people chattering around her. Then she disappeared, then reappeared later."

Jack said, "She could have gone to the bathroom or for snacks."

"Yes, but there were a lot of people at the tables in her way...she had maneuvered through them before, to go to make up and wardrobe checks... but not this time. Then she just reappeared later...And not just her...It happened with other people on other days."

"Look, here she is," Justin pointed to an image on his laptop, "a sweet little old grandmother type... in the corner chair with the book."

Mike peered at the image, "Well, a grandmother from the 1950s maybe. Or from a movie..."

"Not what grandmothers look like today...real but not real," Jack agreed.

"Look at her shoes," Chelsea said as Justin moved on to another image of the woman standing in line with other background waiting to be led to set by a PA.

"A little large, is that it?" Mike asked.

"Yes, and they're brown wingtips..." she noted. Justin moved through a few more images of other figures in the background tent. "Now these other characters, this blond young guy with glasses, this middle-aged plump suit man, this guy in the security guards uniform and this red headed lady...They all did the same vanishing thing. Notice the same shoes on the plus size suit man and the guard."

Mike and Jack both stared and compared, they began to see details that began to make them wonder.

"Jack, looking at all this is reminding me of your dream," Mike said.

Jack nodded, his eyes intent on the various images flicking slowly on the screen as Justin recycled them. "Yes, I think some of these faces were in my dream. There are details that stuck in my mind from seeing them around the set. The red flower on the hat..." Being an artist there were certain kinds of details that stood out to him. "The green of the blond guys glasses frames, the blue of the suit of the plump man..." in his mind he pictured the memories. He had vivid recall. "They were all the same height, all just about my height." Jack was five feet nine, average, he always wished he were taller like

Mike, so he had a heightened awareness of peoples heights. The fact that young people seemed to be increasingly taller these days, (due to eating more protein or maybe drinking more carbonation) added to his sensitivity.

"Exactly!" exclaimed Chelsea, "I noticed it too. Plus the face shape, the eye colors too."

Justin zoomed in to the eyes on them all. "Maybe if this person was changing quickly he or she wouldn't be able to change colored contacts, so couldn't alter that detail."

"Yes, in my dream the phantom had the same eyes..." Jack realized.

"What dream? Tell us about your dream," Chelsea and Justin asked.

As Jack refilled coffees he relayed his recent dream, marveling as he recalled its details, how it synced with what they were now looking at.

Mike meanwhile was continuing to study the images, his mind traveling and sifting possibilities and possible suspects. If this was only one person, a someone adept at make up...someone who might have knowledge of how to access corpses awaiting burial...

"Great work everyone, great observations, " Mike said, "I have an idea. How does everyone feel about checking out some funeral homes?"

"Yikes, do you think the phantom is that deadly? Should we be writing our wills," Justin asked a bit nervously.

"Don't worry, I need your help researching and calling to find out some information about local funeral parlors that may have hired help in recent months. I think there's a connection between our three dead bodies," Mike explained.

"Three dead bodies, I thought there were only two?" Chelsea wondered, "The first one by the lake, the second one in the closet in Miss Zane's suite. Where's the third one?"

Jack and Justin both had the same thought, since both remembered the same pervious event, then Chelsea did too, as they all heard the rumors of trouble on another movie set of Cal Radcliffe's.

"The dead body in LA!" They all said in unison.

"But all three can't have passed through the same funeral home?" Chelsea said.

Detective Mike explained, "No, but the same person could have worked on all three of them in both parts of the country."

Jack said, "Right, and that person would be good with make up. Also they would know what body was stored where and not buried yet..."

"It's spring, wouldn't they have buried everyone by now?" Justin asked.

"You'd be surprised how easily some of the dead can be forgotten," Mike said wistfully.

Chapter 19 - Invisible Visible

Mike had had the director call the crew and cast together on the set of the barroom. He had asked the bookclub members extras to be there as taking their places as they had in their scene... Curious whispers were passing around the room, the waiting cast and crew knew something was going to happen, but no what to expect.

When everything was set, as though they were filming a scene in the movie. The PA called for quiet, then rolling, then action...The small corner stage where the Jessica the movie's murderess had sung was lit with a flattering dramatic spotlight in front of the red velvet stage curtain, it seemed to call for someone to appear.

There was a hush and anxious, expectant whispers...

Mike appeared from the part in the red curtains, looking handsome, stern and bashful, as he began to speak, " Ladies and Gentleman all of you have in one way or another suffered the fearful drama of the phantom of this film..." His voice was deep and grew stronger as he announced, "You will be relieved to know the person responsible has been apprehended. The perpetrator has surrendered voluntarily, and in exchange I promised I would allow him a chance to speak to you all...to apologize and explain."

It was then people noticed his left hand was hidden by the curtain, he drew it forward revealing a pair of arms handcuffed at the wrists, the chrome manacles gleamed in the stage light...

"Are you filming this?" the director whispered to the DP,

"Right from the start." He smiled back at the boss.

"Good man," the director whispered.

As Mike stepped forward he pulled the handcuffed attached person into the spotlight and he stepped back...It was a wiry young man... who looked vaguely familiar to them all... he calmly started to speak, to confess, his confession was really a performance...

Mike thought, "Why not give him his moment, he's not going anywhere. And I am pretty sure Director Barker, he has cameras rolling, so the confession will be captured on film. Though I'm not sure if it will be admissible in court."

The handcuffed young man began in a clear expressive voice, "Ladies and gentlemen, I admit I am the mysterious phantom of your film...

My name is Willam Summers. I confess to my various pranks, but my aim was not to harm anyone but the one man who I seek revenge against. My goal was simple justice against the villain who is a thief and a murderer...the man who seduced my brother, broke his heart and stole his screenplay — degrading him to such a degree that he hung himself. Cal Radcliffe destroyed my family and my career in the process..."

The eyes of the room sought out Cal, who was sitting with a martini playing it cool at the bar. Some were shocked, others were not surprised at all by such an accusation. But everyone was swept up in the theatrical drama of the moment.

The young man's face was washed with despair, "Tragically my brother loved this man, believed he was loved by Radcliffe, that's how sweet and young and foolish he was. He thought his Hollywood dreams were coming true. He was promised his movie project would be brought to life by the star he worshiped and gave himself too.

My brother had never even been with a man before, he gave himself to you." Willam looked towards Cal, "Tom trusted you! You probably thought it was a challenge to get this straight guy not just into bed, but to love you enough that you could take his screenplay. You told him they'd only produce it if your name was on it. Tom was unknown, a nobody, but if he trusted you, you'd see he'd get credit later and that would make his name...

After Tom's death I waited and planed, I got on your sets as an extra. Background extras are invisible, so I was an invisible man... I used multiple disguises and costumes so I could be different, to not be memorable... I watched, listened and saw that you hadn't changed...I saw you using your celebrity to take advantage of other young guys like my brother. Use them and lose them, with your assistant complicit...I have notes, photos, interviews to tell that story to the world.

But revenge took hold like a drug and one deception led to another...I had worked at a funeral home in LA which is how that body got to your set there. It wasn't hard to get taken on part time locally, which gave me access to the gurney to transport the bodies I borrowed from storage. That's how I knew which cemeteries had which bodies waiting...It was always my brother's body I thought of..." his sad eyes shimmered with used tears.

Then an ironic expression clouded his face as he said, "One final thing, I want you to know Cal Radcliffe you will be carrying some of my brother with you in some part, hopefully forever. Because my brother was cremated and I managed to sneak some of his ashes into your coffee and food over the past weeks, so he's inside you and hopefully he will haunt you forever. You ate his soul, it seemed just."

At that moment Cal Radcliffe, turned violently green and dashed from the room to be violently sick.

The composure he had been working hard to retain, his hardened wall of calm, the deflecting the accusations of his accuser by looks that played that this was all mad ranting, was destroyed. His assistant dashed after him wearing a similar horrified expression recalling unwanted drinks of Cal's he had covertly sipped.

The room that had been quietly rapt with attention, suddenly exploded with a cacophony of raucous sounds; gasps of horror, hysterical laughter, even a smattering of applause.

At this point in the confession attention was returned to the stage, as Willam surprisingly began a demonstration of his skills. First as an escape artist showing he'd gotten out of the handcuffs. He announced, "Don't worry, I'm not going to really escape…I promised," he winked at Mike by his side, with whom he'd made a deal to have his time then go with him quietly.

"So I'm not going anywhere, but in a way I am going to disappear…"

Rapidly phantom Willam demonstrated his skill as a quick change artist transforming into the variety of characters that had all been stuffed in his bag.

The audience recognized the various background extras from the past weeks, none of them were him — yet they were all him.

Day after day on the production he had appeared as assorted extras; Jill the blonde, Martin the mustached suit man, Betty the blue haired elder, Brandon the blue haired kid, Peter the bespectacled nerd... even a guard and a PA. His disguises were good, very good. His training in make up along with many helpful Youtube videos on molding subtle facial prosthetics and many other helpful tips to alter your face without detection, allowed Willam to become a merry band of characters. All visible in holding and moving in the background of scenes, yet invisible, having no importance on a movie set. Willam Summers was present and yet largely unnoticed as he (or she) passed here and there on the way the restroom, or craft service or... was looking for wardrobe or make up or hair to as if to get something adjusted.

The phantom had counted on the production team and actors being focused on the filming, not paying attention to things they didn't need to in the intense shooting days. What he hadn't counted on was the observant eyes of Justin, Chelsea, Mike and Jack to each note tiny flaws in his daily performances. Even this might have been all right, if they just stashed the little quirks in the back of their minds...

Now that it was revealed why Willam was carrying out his plot, and indeed a plot it was, planned over time, stealing the bodies with dark humor and darker intentions, because of wrong done to him. He wanted to revenge himself and his brother.

Bizarrely Will believed out of his dark role playing was came some of the best character performances of his life, which ultimately would be peppered through the movie. Certainly the roles he was adapting, changing like a chameleon, were the most varied, at least since he had quit the Laugh Til You Drop Improve troupe...

For each new character Will spoke a few lines in their voice before a flash change to the next one. The stage seemed to briefly almost have the illusion of a small crowd...receiving a round of applause at the end.

The phantom took a small bow.

Suddenly it was over, Will was himself again, now in the role of captured avenger, very captured as at the end of his little performance he found himself once again handcuffed and with leg chains! Detective Mike had used this opportunity to utilize his magician skills. He followed up by dramatically materializing a large black cloak.

Mike explained he also practices magic, and the magic of the law! Suddenly swirling the cloak over Willam Summers, in a puff of smoke he disappeared them both!

"Wow, what a finish!" gasped the camera man. The director fainted with excitement.

Mike allowed the unmasked phantom to take one more quick bow on the street outside the hotel before hustling the criminal into the waiting police car outside.

"Wow," Detective Mike murmured, "being around all this drama has brought out the ham in me...But it was kind of fun."

Chapter 20 - A Party & A Viper Lover

Some days later, with the movie wrapped, and most of the cast and crew off to rest or work on their next project. Meanwhile the film was being edited frantically in LA by the adrenaline crazed director, want to get it to a final cut as quickly as possible, to take advantage of the burst of publicity resulting from the strange phantom of the film.

Mike and Jack were hosting a small gathering they called the AFTERMATH party in the garden of their carriage-house on Nottinghill Lane. Everyone had their drinks and nibbles and were gathered around the large table that had been set up. Conversation had transitioned from here and there between people, to an open form with everyone tossing out remarks to float in the air like bubbles watching and listening to see who might puff out another to add to it or float new… as the shock and awe of the recent events was still being processed by those in attendance. But this green, calm and friendly garden atmosphere allowed a relaxed unbending of nerves and thoughts.

Jack and Mike sat together at the head of the table, and proposed a toast to the end of the film and the beginning of summer.

Jack held his glass up high with a smile, saying, "I am happy to announce the hotel has made enough money from being the location to complete all their refurbishment in time to reopen to the public in a month, finger crossed."

"Oh good, " Jessica exclaimed, "I loved my

suite of rooms there. Well, up until the body fell out of the closet." Everyone laughed.

Jessica and Whitney had rented a lovely cottage right on the beach so they could stay on in the town longer and explore the area over the end of June. They had been so entranced by the miles of white sand beach and almost Mediterranean blue water Mike and Jack had show them in the area.

The chatter was gay at first, but then dimmed at bit as the male star of the films struggles were mentioned.

"Cal Radcliffe was stunned to learn his reliable back bone assistant was a viper in his midst."

"One of the many vipers surrounding him..." Jessica said,

Whitney said, "Some Stars gather darkness, some stars gather light." She glanced loyally at her light star.

"I always thought Malcom was...something was odd, off ...and it was...his inner demon the put all those bad things out on social media. A true troll."

"Such an odd balance to be putting out positive publicity by day, and by night being a spreader or darkness working against himself."

"In the end I think he just became addicted to getting a response..." Whitney said.

Justin offered, "I think he simmered too because, Cal screwed everyone but him. I think he wanted to screw all the guys Cal did, and he was sick of covering it up and jealous at the same time."

"It makes crazy thinking about it, no wonder his mind was twisted into pretzels," Chelsea said, she went on to entertain the guests with reading some of her written accounts of the adventures of the film production, which managed to encompass both dramatic and comic antidotes and observations, at the end she received a round of applause. She took a small bow. "I was doing this as little sketch at first, but now I think I'll end up making it into something more..."

"Very Dickensian, my dear boy, " said the

elderly Howard Earl one of the book club members, though he was really a Poe fan.

Conversation was filed again by Jack and Mike refreshing all the drinks, and fireflies came out as the sun dipped behind the trees. Candles were lit in the center of the table, the evening breeze whispered the trees around them.

Jessica sighed and sipped her whiskey, memory pulled her off down a painful path,"This is a world of strange, show-business. It can make you want to murder. For example, my best part ever was in that bio pic of Ruth eying. An amazing cast, terrific film, but as strangely happens there was another film, another movie about her! At the same time! Some studio back room bargaining went on and my picture got delayed! It was awful. Both were excellent pictures, with both leading actors gave good performances — it was really all down to who came out first! Ann Simons movie premiered first, got the reviews, box office, a god-damned Oscar! If my movie had been able to come out

first it would have been mine! Then some years later she dies of an overdose! So it didn't make her so happy... Well, my picture is still good.
It's a bitch of a business."

No one argued with her. They watched her with admiring eyes, after all she was a movie star, and they still were amazed she was right there amongst them.

Marvelous Miss Zane continued,"And these accidents, they happen often enough on sets, so as not to be all that suspicious. Poor Bart Richards was smashed in the head with a mental chair the first day of Storm Driver, his jaw was never the same; painkillers, addiction, and surgeries. He managed to go on being a star for a long time nonetheless, even Chad Dustin who did all those fun action comedy adventure films, his body has been so abused over those few busy years, jumping off burning boats in the Nile and swinging from vines as a jungle man, he's barely working, and he's still young.

While we woman, not that we don't take ricks

and aren't put endanger too, thrown into freezing water naked take after take, and such. But then we hit a certain age…" She sighed again, looking beautiful and ageless,"No surgery for me…" She brightened, "I've survived this films crazy drama and it's made me feel, I can do most anything!"She raised her glass.

"That's the spirit," Justin said.

"And I have love by my side," she beamed at Whitney who snuggled closer.

"As do I my true-heart," she whispered kissing her hair.

"Here's to love," Justin called out tasing his gas too in a toast, as he slipped his free arm around beaming Hank. Mike and Jack held hands and toasted as well.

Chelsea grinned and raised her camera phone, calling out, "Smile!" Which was really unnecessary as everyone in attendance already was.

Epilogue

Many weeks later, after the film was wrapped and the crazy cross of press and tourists had diminished, the town of Bluewater had gone back to its slower rural pace.

The group of Nottinghill Lane book friends assembled once again at the Inkblot Pub.

"Whenever he gets out of prison Willam Summers will probably end up playing himself in a TV film," Jack said.

Chelsea said, "Well, I think it is kind of great

that he was able to create a murder mystery without actually killing anyone." Murders around the table seemed to agree.

"He'll probably be in a mental institution for a while, and serve sometime," Mike explained.

"That won't hurt his odds in show business, " Jack comment with wry humor.

Mike said,"I'm not sure what all the DA's final charges might be since he didn't actually murder anyone just body snatched... along with acts of vandalism and endangerment. I'm not sure if the brother's ashes in Radcliffe's edibles counts as forced Cannibalism...if there is such a thing. "

Justin who was sitting beside Hank (as was now usually the case) said, "I think Cal Radcliffe deserves what he got, which isn't much, really. He's not in jail, he's still rich, he just has had to disappear as more guys spoke out about his unsavory predatory behavior. I read he was spotted in Spain recently, looking older and puffier."

Hank said, "His ego seemed bulletproof to me,

in my brief encounter."

* * *

It was one of the many oddities of show business that part of the films success came from the publicity of the real life disasters on the set... and all the tabloid and internet tales of the attempted murder and stolen corpses.

Having the cameras rolling capturing many of the eventful dark moments and editing them into the film made it a challenge for audiences to detect what was real and what was staged...

Ironically, Phantom William's various disguised background appearances would become a boost to the film as people made a game of finding him hidden in the various scenes, like the Where's Waldo books. It reminded some of the great actor Alec Guinness in his many murderous disguises in the deadly classic film: Kind Hearts and Coronets.

* * *

In Bluewater City summer kicked into high gear and the swarms of tourists and summer residents were curious about the film they'd read about, the hotel became so popular it was possible the owners could finally get into the black again...

On quiet Nottinghill Lane, Jack's carriage-house studio was humming with various creative spirits;

Hank went back to continuing the garden additions he was working on. Now with Justin's occasional help, when he wasn't busy looking over Chelsea's shoulder and making suggestions, as she spent a great deal of time in the walled garden writing about all that had recently happened.

Jack went happily back to his painting, getting ready to take part in an exhibition in the fall. Mike when he could posed for him, almost naked, his body looking as succulent and lean as ever.

"One day we'll be reading and talking over Chelsea's book about this spring's movie mystery in the book club," Jack said to Mike as he applied brushstrokes to the canvas in front of him.

"I can't wait, I'm looking forward to it, she has a unique way with words," Mike said with a saucy smile curling his delectable lips, "there's something else I'm looking forward to, when ever you feel like taking a break…"

"Hey, be patient! Great art takes time," Jack shot Mike an amused glance.

"Great art, I'm glad your beginning to believe in your talent more," Mike said.

"Great art, with great inspiration," Jack chuckled, as his eyes swept over his lover's chiseled body, with the golden afternoon sun layering it like honey, he thought he might need to take a break very soon.

BOOK: The Naked Detective & the Movies
- A Book and Page, Nottinghill Lane Mystery
Copyright © 2019 by guy veryzer

Warning: The unauthorized reproduction or distribution of this copyrighted work is illegal. Criminal copyright infringement, including infringement without monetary gain, is investigated by the FBI and is punishable by up to 5 (five) years in federal prison and a fine of $250,000.

Names, characters and incidents depicted in this book are products of the author's imagination or are used fictitiously. Any resemblance to actual events, locales, organizations, or persons, living or dead, is entirely coincidental and beyond the intent of the author or the publisher.

No part of this book may be reproduced or transmitted in any form or by any means, electronic or mechanical, including photocopying, recording, or by any information storage and retrieval system, without permission in writing from the author.

Cover Photos: Shutterstock Inc.   Cover Design: Guy Veryzer

bowie15 credit istock for blond guy

wrangel credit for dark haired guy